Her Adorable Cad

The Worthington Legacy
Book Three

Marie Higgins

© Copyright 2024 by Marie Higgins
Text by Marie Higgins
Cover by Kim Killion Designs

Dragonblade Publishing, Inc. is an imprint of Kathryn Le Veque Novels, Inc.

P.O. Box 23
Moreno Valley, CA 92556
ceo@dragonbladepublishing.com

Produced in the United States of America

First Edition April 2024
Trade Paperback Edition

Reproduction of any kind except where it pertains to short quotes in relation to advertising or promotion is strictly prohibited.

All Rights Reserved.

The characters and events portrayed in this book are fictitious. Any similarity to real persons, living or dead, is purely coincidental and not intended by the author.

ARE YOU SIGNED UP FOR DRAGONBLADE'S BLOG?

You'll get the latest news and information on exclusive giveaways, exclusive excerpts, coming releases, sales, free books, cover reveals and more.

Check out our complete list of authors, too!

No spam, no junk. That's a promise!

Sign Up Here
www.dragonbladepublishing.com

Dearest Reader;

Thank you for your support of a small press. At Dragonblade Publishing, we strive to bring you the highest quality Historical Romance from some of the best authors in the business. Without your support, there is no 'us', so we sincerely hope you adore these stories and find some new favorite authors along the way.

Happy Reading!

CEO, Dragonblade Publishing

Additional Dragonblade books by Author Marie Higgins

The Worthington Legacy
Her Perfect Scoundrel (Book 1)
Her Dreamy Deceiver (Book 2)
Her Adorable Cad (Book 3)

Love's Addiction Series
A Wallflower to Love (Book 1)
A Governess to Protect (Book 2)
A Maiden to Remember (Book 3)

What more can the second daughter of a penniless lord hope to gain in life than becoming the companion to the Dowager Duchess of Englewood? Especially when she was resigned to being a spinster. However, misfortune strikes Priscilla Hartwell's world once again when the rogue who has broken her heart returns and brings more havoc. She is determined not to let him steal her heart again. Yet, against her will, she finds she is drawn to him now more than ever before.

Chapter One

Heaven has no rage like love to hatred turned / nor hell a fury like a woman scorned.

WILLIAM CONGREVE'S PLAY, *The Mourning Bride*, had been on Priscilla Hartwell's mind for two years now. She'd experienced firsthand what it was like to have not one, but two men reject her outright and leave her heartbroken and desolate. She had become a spinster at the age of twenty-four. If only she could have been fortunate like her older sister, Bridget, who had married the perfect man who could support her well.

Priscilla pulled her thoughts out of the past and focused on what was currently happening. The jarring coach she had been riding in for several hours now was gnawing on her already tattered nerves. She had accepted a position as the Dowager Duchess of Englewood's lady's companion.

Although anxious to move ahead with her life, Priscilla especially wanted to get away from her father, who was ruining the hopes and dreams of every one of his children, as he expected them to marry someone wealthy instead of for love. Once she realized she would never marry because of having no dowry, she was satisfied to be the companion to the dowager duchess.

Now Priscilla would get to wear nicer gowns instead of ones that had been altered every year since she was fourteen. Finally, she would be able to hold her head high at Society's functions without the fear of someone gossiping about her poor family and how the Hartwell daughters were only after men with money.

The Dowager Duchess of Englewood was in her early sixtieth year and really didn't need a companion, but she was very good friends with Priscilla's grandmother—and so the deal was made that Priscilla would live with the dowager, who was crippled and confined to a rollerchair.

The rhythm of the coach slowed, and Priscilla peered out the window at the magnificent three-story estate as they approached. It was very similar to the one Bridget was living in with her adoring husband, Lord Adrian Worthington. The grounds were immaculately cared for, and so very green. There was even a flower garden off toward the back of the estate that was visible. She hoped the dowager would allow her to spend time in the gardens.

Priscilla smiled. Perhaps good fortune was indeed smiling upon her, just in a different way.

She clutched her satchel and scooted closer to the door. The dowager had sent her own coach decorated with the family's crest of blue and silver on the door. Priscilla had never felt so regal in her life. She prayed this wouldn't be the last time she enjoyed this special emotion. She needed more of it, and often.

The coach stopped and a footman opened the door. He helped her down before lifting her trunk off the back of the coach. She walked up the several steps toward the estate. A butler wearing a black and red uniform waited at the open door, and when he saw her, he bowed slightly.

"Welcome to Englewood Hall. I am Martin. We have been expecting you." He motioned to her satchel. "I will have that taken to your room."

Priscilla smiled at the older man and handed the satchel to another footman who stood nearby. The butler's pure white hair was still full, which surprised her, since he appeared to be in his sixties. He was very dignified in his later years, and she thought he was quite pleasant.

"I thank you for your welcome, Martin."

"The Dowager Duchess of Englewood is waiting for you in the sitting room, Miss Priscilla. If you will follow me, I shall take you to her."

"Of course."

Nervously, she wrung her hands as she followed the butler. The tiled floors were polished to perfection, and every lamp, table, and picture was impeccably dusted. Living in this manor would be like living in a museum, but it would be a relief not to have to clean and cook, as she had done for several years, since their father made very little money and she and her sisters had to do the duties of a servant.

As she followed the butler into the sitting room, immediately she recognized the dowager duchess. The bony, shriveled old woman with silvery-white hair sat hunched in her cushioned chair, staring toward the hearth. Low flames danced on the burned log as bits of smoke curled up toward the chimney.

"Your Grace, Miss Priscilla is here," Martin announced.

The older woman's back straightened slightly and she turned. When the woman's gaze landed on Priscilla, her eyes widened and she smiled, enhancing her many wrinkles, but her brown eyes sparkled like stars.

"Miss Priscilla." She motioned with her hand. "Come here so I can see you better. I don't have my spectacles at the moment, so you are a blur."

After curtsying, Priscilla grinned and moved closer. "It's so nice to see you again, Your Grace. Grandmother Hartwell speaks so highly of you. I feel as if I know you already."

The duchess nodded and took hold of Priscilla's hands. "Your grandmother is such a dear friend. I'm so happy to have one of her granddaughters as my companion." She squinted and peered toward the butler. "Martin? Will you ask Mrs. Jones to have tea brought in?"

"Yes, Your Grace."

Priscilla was tempted to get the tea service ready herself—

since that was what she had done at home—but she quickly stopped herself. She must remember she was the companion of a duchess and not her servant.

The dowager patted the armrest of the sofa next to her. "Please sit so we can chat. There are so many things I would like to know about you."

Nodding, Priscilla sat on the sofa and folded her hands on her lap. "I, too, have many questions. Although I'm sure I'll learn quickly, I don't know how to be a companion to a duchess."

The older lady chuckled. "Keeping me entertained is probably the thing you will do the most. Your grandmother told me you play the pianoforte quite well, and since I love music, I'm sure I'll ask you to play for me many times throughout the day." She glanced down at her crooked fingers and sighed heavily. "I used to play well myself, but old age is taking over my body quickly."

"I absolutely love playing the pianoforte." Priscilla beamed. "Would you like me to play something for you now?"

"Indeed. Help me into my chair and take me to the music room."

As Priscilla assisted the dowager into the rollerchair, she recalled when she had first heard about the chair with wheels that her father's distant cousin, John Dawson of Bath, had invented for invalids. The chair, which had two large wheels behind and one in front, had made him very rich. Her father constantly cursed his cousin for not sharing some of that wealth with the penniless relatives. Then again, if she were John, she wouldn't give her father money either, since he rarely spent it on his children.

They reached the music room, and Priscilla helped the dowager out of the rollerchair and to the sofa. As she stepped to the pianoforte, her mind was already putting together a memorized piece that she enjoyed playing. Once she sat on the stool, her fingers moved over the keys as if they had a mind of their own, for indeed they did. Her enjoyment for music was evident in the way she played.

Playing had always soothed her, but at the moment, she

couldn't keep memories from resurfacing. She had captured the attention of two men over the past six years because of how well she played. The first had been Collin, Lord Hanover, who had inherited the new title of Lord Kentwood and was now happily married. But less than eighteen months ago, she had attended one of her aunt's dinner parties, where she was given the opportunity to play. Viscount Lennox had been in attendance. His dashing good looks and charming manner had swept many women off their feet, but the dirty, rotten cad had picked her as his next target.

When the volume of the music increased, her thoughts turned to how the viscount had gazed at her with his smoldering green eyes and kissed her hand with his gentle lips. He had tried several times to meet her in private, but something had always complicated their plans. At the time, she had been quite put out by the interruptions. Now, she was grateful nothing had happened between them. Gavin's attention was easily diverted to another innocent female, and he never spoke to Priscilla again.

The viscount had been just like Lord Hanover. The two lords—who were, incidentally, cousins—knew exactly how to twist up her feelings and shatter her hopes of ever finding a man to marry. Of course, it was her family's misfortune that turned her into a spinster.

She finished Mozart's piece and rested her hands in her lap. Her whole body shook from the disappointment and anger rushing through her. As the dowager clapped enthusiastically, Priscilla took in deep breaths, trying to calm her ire.

"Oh, Miss Priscilla, you played wonderfully and dramatically. Indeed, your grandmother did not exaggerate about your special talent. I don't believe I have witnessed a better performance than the one you just gave. *Brava*, my dear."

Finally feeling as if she had rid herself of heartbreaking memories, Priscilla faced the woman and smiled. "I thank you for your generous compliment, Your Grace. I fear I tend to let my feelings go when I'm playing."

A cheery woman, perhaps in her late thirties, brought in a tray filled with teacups, a teakettle, and a plate of crumpets. The woman's red curls bounced as she walked. She gave a nod to Priscilla before placing the tray on the nearby table.

"Thank you, Mrs. Jones." The duchess motioned to the servant. "Miss Priscilla, this is my housekeeper. She and my cook know what types of food I enjoy during certain times of the day, and it just so happens that this is when I eat my crumpets. I hope you don't mind."

Priscilla smiled at the dowager. "Not at all. I enjoy crumpets as well." She shifted her attention to the housekeeper. "I'm happy to make your acquaintance, Mrs. Jones."

The servant curtsied. "It's nice to meet you, Miss Priscilla." She turned back to the duchess. "Your favorite grandson just arrived. He is wondering if he can visit with you."

The dowager beamed. "Of course he can. I can't wait to introduce him to my companion."

The housekeeper nodded. "Would you like me to pour your tea first?"

"No, Miss Priscilla can pour it. You hurry and fetch that handsome grandson of mine. I haven't seen him since he took over his new title two months ago."

"Yes, Your Grace." The servant curtsied before hurrying out the door.

Without a word, Priscilla moved to the tray and began pouring the tea. In her mind, she pictured the duchess's grandson to be a scrawny young man, probably just getting ready to enter Eton. But the footsteps coming into the room seemed heavier on the hardwood floor than a young man's would.

The duchess clapped her hands. "Oh, there you are, my boy. Come over here and give your lonely grandmother a big hug."

Priscilla was glad to hear that the duchess greeted her grandchildren just the way her own grandmother greeted the family. Once the tea was poured, she straightened and turned toward the woman.

"Grams, I don't dare give you a hug. During my ride, I stopped to assist a carriage that had driven off the road, and I don't want to transfer the dust from my clothes to yours."

The dowager gasped. "They were off the road? How terrible. I pray they were not harmed."

From where she stood, Priscilla could only see the back of him, and although his clothes were scuffed up a bit with dirt and mud, one thing was certain—this man was *not* scrawny or very young at all. His shoulders were wide and the rest of him looked muscular.

Her face heated from her inappropriate thoughts. She really need not think in that manner. After all, what good would it do her?

"It is nothing to be worried about, I assure you, and nobody was harmed," he said, kissing his grandmother on the cheek. "I must say, you look prettier every time I see you."

"Oh, posh! You certainly need spectacles." The duchess giggled and playfully swatted his arm. "My dear boy, you have to meet my new companion."

The man straightened and turned toward Priscilla. Just as she met his gaze, and she took in the structure of his handsome face and wavy, dark hair, recognition struck. Rejection tugged at her heart just as painfully as it had eighteen months ago. Panic gripped her throat, squeezing tightly. She lost her breath, and she feared she might swoon. But no! She would not give him the satisfaction of seeing her lose consciousness just because she was shocked speechless.

It couldn't be Gavin Worthington. A small gasp broke through her tight throat before she had time to stop it. Why didn't she know Viscount Lennox was the duchess's grandson?

Apparently, he was just as surprised, because recognition showed in his wide eyes. Within seconds, his jovial smile disappeared.

The duchess tapped her grandson's arm. "Gavin, I would like to introduce you to my new lady's companion, Miss Priscilla

Hartwell. Miss Priscilla, this is my grandson, the newly appointed Duke of Englewood."

A knot tightened in Priscilla's belly. He was a duke? How could such a rotten man be given a noble title? Gavin didn't deserve it.

Priscilla's head began spinning and her stomach lurched. She held her breath and tried to keep from embarrassing herself all over the carpet. If Gavin was the duke, did that mean he would preside over this estate? She prayed not. She didn't think she could tolerate a rogue like him. She would certainly lose her position with the duchess, and she was sure she wouldn't ever find work again.

Perhaps it was best to bite her tongue and not make a scene. But could she do it when all she wanted to do right now was scream at him and slap his deceitful face? Maybe she would kick him in the shins, or a place on his body that would hurt him as much as his treatment of her eighteen months ago had injured her heart.

GAVIN STARED AT Priscilla, and his mind drew a blank on what to say to her. Seeing her after all this time was such a surprise, and he didn't know how to act. He certainly remembered their brief time together, but once they parted ways, he had quickly forgotten the lovely Hartwell sister. Over his many years of charming women, none of them had stayed on his mind for very long before he tired of them.

However, she seemed to have changed since they were together last. He recalled her being shy, almost as if she was afraid of her own shadow. It had been her innocence, her intense blue eyes, and her soft voice that had first attracted him. Being an expert at charming women, he had wanted to achieve the thrill of seduction with Miss Priscilla. He had thought to turn her from the plain, ordinary girl she had presented into a butterfly.

But now there was no resemblance of the ordinary girl he had known. Instead, she was a fully grown woman with delicate facial features and pretty black hair coiled up in a bun while wisps were left loose around her ears and near her temples. The gown she wore hugged her bosom, emphasizing that she had indeed developed into a lovely woman. He now wondered why he didn't see that before. Could a woman really change that much in a year and a half?

There was only one word to describe her now. *Breathtaking.*

She blinked and lowered her gaze to the floor as she curtsied. "It's a pleasure to see you again, Your Grace."

Gavin had only had the title for a few months, but he didn't think he would ever get used to hearing *Your Grace*. After all, that had been his father's title before he died.

Remembering his manners, he bowed slightly. "Oh, no. The pleasure is all mine, Miss Priscilla. I'm very glad you are here to help my grandmother. I'm sure she appreciates you as much as I do."

"It is I who appreciates the opportunity, Your Grace," she said as she looked at his grandmother.

"You two know each other?" Grandmother asked, switching her gaze back and forth between them.

"Yes," Gavin answered. "We met over a year ago at her aunt's dinner party."

"Oh, how lovely," Grandmother said with a bounce to her voice. "Then I'm sure you were able to hear Miss Priscilla play the pianoforte. She is magnificent."

Priscilla wasn't meeting his eyes, but her cheeks turned pink from his grandmother's compliment. "Yes, Grandmother. I did hear her play, and she was indeed magnificent."

"I thank you, Your Grace." Priscilla cleared her throat and turned toward the tea service. "Would you like some tea?"

"I appreciate your thinking of me, but I must decline." He bent and kissed his grandmother's cheek again. "Please forgive me, but I have a meeting with my solicitor, and after stopping to help a carriage, I fear I'm in great need of cleaning myself up."

"Of course, dear." The dowager patted his arm. "But I hope you will make me happy and be here for dinner."

"Yes, of course." He grinned. "I have missed your company." As he took a step toward the door, he glanced at Priscilla again. "I shall see you later."

She nodded and quickly turned away as she took a cup of tea to his grandmother. But he clearly noticed how her expression hardened.

After he left the music room and closed the door, he scowled. Obviously, Miss Priscilla was going to give him the cold shoulder for a while. He probably deserved it. After all, he had only been after one thing while he charmed her all those many months ago, and when he couldn't even elicit a kiss from her, he had given up and moved on. However, he felt she had started to like him.

Blowing out a breath of frustration, he climbed the stairs and headed for his bedchamber. He hadn't planned on staying long at the manor, but now he was rethinking the length of his visit. He couldn't leave now knowing that Miss Priscilla loathed him. He must make amends somehow.

A memory popped into his head, and he recalled how nicely she had fit in his arms. He had enjoyed her softness pressing intimately against him. But now, she was so much more a woman than before, and he wondered how she would feel next to him while sharing a passionate kiss.

His heart leapt. Good grief! Perhaps it wasn't wise to imagine them entwined in such a way. And it certainly wasn't a good idea to think that the art of seduction looked better and better with this particular woman. But he was no longer that man. His rogue days were behind him, and although it would be foreign to him, he must present himself as a respectable duke, not only for his frame of mind, but because Miss Priscilla deserved to be treated like the lady she was.

Chapter Two

Although the dowager retired to bed early, Priscilla could not. Her mind was still wide awake. She had stressed herself sick right before dinner, not wanting to see Gavin again, but then the inconsiderate rogue hadn't shown up. Instead, he sent his grandmother a note stating that his meeting was running longer. The old woman laughed it off, telling Priscilla that Gavin had become a busy man since he stepped into his new title.

She knew the real reason he hadn't come. He was afraid to face her, and it had nothing to do with his feeling guilty. Men like that had cold hearts.

She sighed and sat on the edge of her mattress, glancing around her bedchamber. The dowager had been very generous with Priscilla's accommodations. She had received so much more than expected for working as a lady's companion. Never in Priscilla's wildest dreams could she have imagined living in such a grand room. It was spacious enough for a large bed and two armoires, and two small, cushioned chairs and a table. Not only that, the room had two windows and an adjoining room for her to bathe.

However, she had nothing to do in this room but gaze at the lovely furnishings and be grateful that she had been chosen to be the companion of a duchess. She needed something to occupy her thoughts so that thoughts of Gavin didn't consume her. She recalled seeing a library during her tour of the manor, and now she wanted to find a book to read. Perhaps that would relax her enough to sleep tonight.

She left her bedchamber holding a lit candle and strolled down the corridor, listening for any signs that Gavin had returned from his meeting. Thankfully, the house was quiet. She couldn't even hear the servants.

With each step down the grand staircase, she gained more assurance that Gavin was still out. She hoped the shock of seeing her had scared him away for good. Of course, she expected him to visit his grandmother on special occasions, just as any good grandson would, but no more than that. And if she saw him again, she wouldn't hold back her verbal disgust of the rogue, especially his ill treatment of her when they last met.

Not that it would change him. He was set in his ways. But perhaps showing him her anger would be the first step to healing her own heart.

Seeing him again after all this time stunned her, and she had wanted to crawl in a hole and hide. But now she was ready to let him know that his nearness didn't bother her any longer. She didn't care what he did with his miserable life, as long as he didn't plan on including her in it.

The lower floor of the manor seemed draftier than it had earlier. She rubbed her arms, certain the fireplaces were extinguished by now, which was why the corridor was cooler. The old manor creaked, and although it startled her, she knew nobody else was awake. Yet prickles rose on her arms, as if someone was watching her.

She rolled her eyes. She was not the type of woman to let creaks frighten her, and she certainly didn't believe in ghosts. Within a week, she would be used to the large manor, and feel much better about wandering through the spacious rooms by herself.

Priscilla opened the large door to the library and held up her candle. She stopped at the nearest upright table and turned up the lamp to brighten the room. The small flame from the candle wouldn't be helpful when trying to find the right book for tonight's reading. Although she really should have gotten a book while the sun's rays were still pouring through the windows earlier today, she had been kept busy with the dowager.

She set her candle on the table before picking up the lamp and stepped closer to the shelves lined with leather-bound books. As she moved from one aisle to the next, she didn't know if she would be able to find something tonight at all. She loved reading, and there were just too many books to choose from.

When she passed a familiar title, she stopped and stared at a copy of William Congreve's *The Mourning Bride*. She chuckled, happy to know that she wasn't a woman scorned anymore. Well… not that much, anyway.

"Why do you find drama so humorous?"

The deep voice behind her made her jump and drop the lamp. The moment it fell to the floor, the light went out. Although she couldn't see him, as she was too far away from her candle, she knew he was very close.

His low laugh irritated her, and if she could see his face, she would be severely tempted to slap it.

"I suppose," he said with a touch of humor, "that I need to rethink sneaking up on women when they are holding a lamp in a dark room."

It irritated her that she hadn't noticed him. The library door had been closed, and no lights were lit. So why would he be hiding in a dark room? If she had known Gavin had returned, she would have stayed in her bedchamber.

"Forgive me, Your Grace, but you startled me. I didn't know there was anyone else in the room, especially this late at night."

"If you must know, I was actually on the other end of the library with a low-burning candle, so I doubt you would have been able to notice me at all."

As her eyes adjusted, she realized there was a small amount of light coming from the end bookcase. "Again, please forgive me for not seeing you. With the lamp, I wouldn't have noticed another light in the room."

"I just hope the flame doesn't go out before I make my way back to that section of the room. After all, the flame was very low."

Her heartbeat quickened. Being in a dark room with him was *not* a good idea. "Yes, please see if you can retrieve it so we can relight the lamp."

She heard the sound of cloth rubbing against cloth mere seconds before he touched her arm. She jumped back, knocking the bookcase.

"Don't be afraid," he said. "I'm just trying to grasp your hand and take you with me."

"Whatever for?" Fear clutched her throat. "I assure you, I'm fine right here."

"You are… unless my candle goes out. Then we shall both be in trouble, because I don't think I know my way around the library in the dark." He touched her arm again and slid his hand down to find her fingers. "I'll try not to lead you into any walls." He chuckled.

Oh, the nerve of that man. Of course he would lead her astray. Their past had already told her she couldn't trust him. Why did he think that had changed? "You, sir, I do not trust."

He laughed. "Indeed? After all this time? We know each other well enough, do we not?"

Priscilla gritted her teeth. *The fool!* She really wished he hadn't brought up that subject. Did he even know what he had unleashed inside her by bringing up their past? If only she could just forgive and forget. But that was easier said than done.

"Yes, we know each other," she bit out slowly as she pulled her hand from his, "which is the very reason I cannot trust you."

He sighed heavily. "Don't tell me you are still upset at me. That was almost two years ago."

"Actually, it was eighteen months," she snapped, and then scolded herself for even saying it. Now he was going to think she had been counting the days, and of course she had not.

"I was close," he mumbled.

Priscilla held herself back from spouting a rude comment. Now was not the time. When she voiced her thoughts, she wanted to watch his expression. She wanted to see if he felt guilty for what had happened between them.

"The point is," she said, more calmly, "I don't trust you and I never will. However, at the moment we have a bigger dilemma. We need to get out of this dark room, which means we need to find your candle or return to the door and retrieve mine."

"And in doing so," he said, grasping her hand again, "we should go together. Besides, my candle is closer."

His warm palm against hers made her body quiver. The dryness of her throat would be obvious if she tried to speak again, and she wasn't about to explain herself to him. The quicker they could get out of here, the better.

Taking slow steps, she blindly followed. From the sounds around her, she could tell he was feeling his way along the wall of the bookcase, because occasionally a book would fall off the shelf. After taking about ten steps, he stopped and turned toward her. Thankfully, she caught herself before bumping against his chest.

"You never did answer my question," he said.

He was close enough for her to smell his minty breath… which was entirely too close. "What—" She cleared her throat. "What question was that?"

"If you are still upset with me."

She breathed deeply, trying to calm her growing ire. "I didn't know that was a question, Your Grace. It sounded more like a statement."

"You are correct, Miss Priscilla, so let me try it again. Are you still upset with me from when we met before?"

"Really, Your Grace, there is no use talking about this. It's in the past, where I would like it to stay."

"Please, call me Gavin." He touched her cheek. "I believe we know each other well enough to be on a first-name basis."

The stroke of his fingers against her cheek startled her, and yet the gentleness of the action had her heart racing out of control. She lifted a trembling hand to push away his touch, but when her fingers connected with his, he took her hand, lifted it to his mouth, and brushed a kiss across her knuckles.

"Cilla," he whispered, "if you don't mind, I would like to start over again. The man you met at your aunt's party no longer exists. I have changed drastically since then."

"Nobody can change so drastically." Her voice warbled.

"Recent events in my life have made it happen, I assure you."

She wasn't sure she liked his nickname for her, but what bothered her more was the way he tried to charm her. Never again would she give him her heart. "Can a leopard change its spots? I think not, Your Grace."

Chuckling, he lowered her hand from his mouth. "And now I'm a leopard? You think I'm fast and powerful?"

"Actually, I would like to retract that comment. Instead, if I were to give you an animal's identity, I would label you a snake."

He laughed, but she detected a hint of injury in his tone. If only she could see his face.

"A *snake*? You think I'm scaly?"

"What I think, Your Grace, is that you are the lowest form of creature that slithers on the ground. You care not for other people's feelings, only care about yourself and your pleasures." She moistened her throat. "If you are looking for another woman to seduce, please search somewhere else. I will not be that foolish again."

"You wound me, my Cilla. Will you not give me the chance to prove that I have changed?"

Was he actually *begging* her? Perhaps it was a good thing he couldn't see her face right now, because it was hard to keep the grin of victory from stretching her mouth from ear to ear. "I suppose. The first thing you could do to prove to me you are no longer the cad I remember is to get us out of this dark room—and without trying to make me swoon with your false flattery."

"As you wish, Miss Priscilla."

He continued in his quest to find the candle, and this time, she was more confident that he would get them across the large library without running into anything—and withholding his flirtations from her, which she suspected was the most difficult for him to do.

Taking small steps, she followed him, and gradually the room became a little brighter. At least she could see the outline of his body. But even once they reached the candle, she was certain there would still be shadows all around them.

Finally, they moved around a bookcase, and she could see the low flame of the candle. She breathed easier and pulled her hand away from his grasp. She took another step closer to the light, and something small and quick ran past her foot. Looking down, she only saw shadows. But shivers climbed over her. Was it a *rodent*?

She shrieked and grasped Gavin's arm, trying to use him to block whatever had scurried past her foot. He reacted by slipping his arm around her waist and holding her against him.

"What is amiss?" he asked.

"Something… something…" She shivered again, wanting nothing more than to get her feet off the ground in case the rodent decided to run by her again. "Something ran by my feet."

"What was it?"

"I don't know. It is too dark to see, but I think it was a mouse. No… it was larger than a mouse. Probably a rat."

She shivered once more as she continued to cling to him, burying her face against his chest. If only she was near a chair or a table, she would crawl on that instead.

"Cilla, please calm yourself." He stroked his large, comforting hand over her back. "I doubt it was a rat. I have never seen one inside my grandmother's estate."

"Then… what was it?" Her voice lifted as panic continued to unsettle her.

He wrapped both arms around her, and oddly enough, the urgency to climb on top of something quickly left her. Slowly, she lifted her head and peeked at his face. Because of the shadows surrounding them, it was difficult to see his expression fully, but concern was etched in the lines on his forehead and around his mouth.

"My darling Cilla, it was probably my grandmother's cat."

"A *cat?*" She felt her heartbeat skip, knowing she should not be in his arms this way—or any way, for that matter. "I have not seen a cat this whole time."

"Miss McKenzie likes to wander around at night and sleep during the day. That is probably why you haven't seen her."

"Miss McKenzie? Is that the cat's name?"

"Yes. Why? Haven't you heard my grandmother mention that name?"

Slowly, Priscilla nodded. "Twice, but I figured it was one of her friends."

"Make no mistake, Miss McKenzie is indeed one of the dowager's friends. Grandmother talks about her pet as if it were a person and not an animal."

Feeling more relaxed, Priscilla smiled. "My grandmother does that with her dog."

While one of his hands still held her against him, he moved the other hand and cupped the side of her face. His thumb stroked her cheek.

"Do you feel better now?"

Realizing she was still intimately pressed against him, she snapped out of the enchantment he had somehow put her under. How could she have allowed him to hold her so personally? Earlier, she had assumed that nothing frightened her. She was mistaken. She was frightened of rodents... and Gavin.

She wiggled out of his hold and stepped back. Now that the contact had been broken between them, she felt a considerable difference in the rhythm of her heartbeat. Not only that, but the warmth that had been flowing through her body had disappeared, leaving her cold and weak.

"I... I think we need to leave this room."

"Have you found a book to read?"

"No, but I shall make that a priority during the day, while I have the sun peeking through the windows to help me look."

"You can read mine." He bent to snatch it from off the nearby sofa. "I have read it many times already." He handed it to her. "If you enjoy mystery novels, you will not be able to put this one down."

Priscilla nearly laughed. Her sister, Bridget, would have claimed this book quickly. Priscilla enjoyed mysteries, but she would rather read a novel with romance. "Thank you." She took it from him.

He picked up the candle. "The flame is almost out. We had better hurry back to your candle, since we didn't think to bring the lamp with us."

Inwardly, she groaned. How could she have forgotten something so vital?

Without asking, he took hold of her hand and pulled her with him. This time, they stepped faster. Once they reached the door, she pulled away. She really should have done that first. Being with him and allowing him to touch her was not a good thing at all. Even now, her mind and heart were playing tug-of-war. Thankfully, the wounds of her heart were still fresh from when he'd trampled on it before.

She had learned her lesson, and she vowed she would never make that mistake again. No matter how hard he tried to convince her he had changed, she would stay strong and remind herself that leopards couldn't change their spots, and snakes would always be loathsome.

Chapter Three

GAVIN STUDIED THE calculations in each column as he budgeted the ledgers, and shook his head. He wasn't fit to be a duke, especially when he didn't want to think about the three estates he had to manage, not to mention the two townhouses, and all the servants that went with them. Although this was now his responsibility, he realized the burden was heavier than he could bear, especially when, as each day passed, he discovered bigger problems.

The meeting with his secretary yesterday had left Gavin puzzled. Jacob McGuire said the oddest thing, which made Gavin want to throw up his arms in surrender. Apparently, the man had heard that Gavin was close to going to debtors' prison.

He had laughed at the family friend's comment, thinking the man was being humorous. But Jacob reported hearing rumors that Gavin's father had given him a depleting inheritance because of unwise investments. This, of course, made him delve into the ledgers, and just as the rumors predicted, he was losing money. If he couldn't think of a way to quickly change things around and start earning, he would lose everything. It appeared as if his father had been more ill in the head before his death than first suspected.

Grumbling, Gavin pushed away from his desk and moved to the window to gaze out on the spring morning. He would thoroughly enjoy spending time outdoors, since the weather appeared quite lovely today. Sadly, the disturbing news about his inheritance had ruined everything, and he cursed his parents. Why hadn't they better prepared him for situations like this? But it was as if the duke's responsibilities had been dumped on him and that everyone around him expected him to know how to fix it. He didn't want to admit how worthless he felt from the overwhelming issue, especially when he had no clue how to dig himself out of this frustrating mess.

Gavin released a defeated sigh and leaned against the window. Another thing that bothered him was that he hadn't been able to meet with his friends and cousins at the gaming tables for two months. Of course, he didn't go there just to gamble. Catching up with these men was much needed, especially during this uncertain time in his life.

He was determined to find the person stealing from his coffers. He also needed to bring the family's name back into good standing. So why were obstacles constantly being thrown in his way? Apparently, this was his penance for those rogue years when he had not cared about anybody but himself. He especially never cared about a woman's feelings.

Miss Priscilla Hartwell's hadn't been the first heart he had broken. There was Miss Madeline Parker, who had bored him to tears, so he seduced her best friend, Lady Georgina Grisham. Miss Jane Eggert was the daughter of a penniless baron, and Gavin had convinced her that they would run off to Gretna Green and marry. Jane was older than him, but at the time, all he wanted was what most rogues wanted... another notch on their bedpost.

Groaning, he scrubbed a hand over his jaw. Perhaps he shouldn't have said that to a woman who had been so desperate to find a husband.

He glanced back at his desk and the ledgers spread across the top. Hopefully, between him and his secretary, they would find the reason money was disappearing and be able to pinpoint the culprit. Until then, Gavin wouldn't be able to feel settled. But for now, he must think of other things, or he would turn insane with frustration.

Immediately, his thoughts shifted to the lovely woman with black hair and a feisty temperament that was now his grandmother's companion. He recalled their time in the dark library last night, and smiled. He found the time spent with her had been rather enjoyable. He couldn't remember ever being with a woman in a library without kissing—or more—happening. Yet nothing improper had transpired during the evening, except that he hadn't been able to stop smiling after they went their separate ways.

He doubted Priscilla shared his enthusiasm.

As he returned to his desk and sat, he found himself grinning wider than expected for having such a rotten morning. Then again, thinking how he had felt like a knight in shining armor with Priscilla in the library made him want to find other ways to change her mind about him. He really could have just picked up the lamp and restarted the kindle, since he had done it many times. But instead, he'd made her believe they had to walk across the library for his candle in order to find their way out of the large room.

Gavin leaned back in his chair and pushed aside the ledgers in front of him. He couldn't concentrate on this. Not now, with so many other things filling his mind.

As a boy, he and his older cousins had played in his grandmother's library. At an early age, they all learned their way around that particular room without knocking anything off the shelves. Sometimes they played games with blindfolds just to see who was better at moving through the small maze of shelves without running into anything.

Of course, he wouldn't make Priscilla aware of this. She would hate him for sure.

Gavin sighed in defeat. He knew he couldn't stay in his study another moment. He left the room and let his long strides take him to the nearest door so that he could be outside, enjoying this beautiful day. He had always been the outdoorsman type. Even as a boy, he had spent more time riding his horse than working on his studies.

He walked to the stable and had his horse prepared to ride. He would stay around the estate today, although he enjoyed riding for hours most days. But certainly, being one with the horse and nature would clear his mind.

The groom brought his horse out, and Gavin mounted. Immediately, he pushed the steed fast, loving the feel of the air against his face. His mind opened, and he recalled when he had gone riding as a young boy. Being an only child, his closest friends were his cousins, but because they didn't live close by, he relied on his horse to listen to his problems and gripes. If only the animal had responded with something rather than a neigh.

Gavin chuckled. As a boy, he thought that by wishing on a star, it would make the animals talk. What a wild imagination he'd had.

As a young adult, he was confident enough to ride to visit his closet cousins—three brothers, Trevor, Tristan, and Trey Worthington. Trey had been his favorite, and closest to Gavin in age. When they reached their maturity, both men became experienced rogues. Indeed, Gavin had learned from the best, even though now he wished he had not been taught to treat women with disrespect. He couldn't count how many hearts he had broken. He really should apologize to Priscilla, if she would only listen. Hopefully, one day she might find it in her heart to forgive him.

Once again, the image of her face popped into his mind, and surprisingly, he found himself anxious to see her again, even though he knew she was mad at him. But it didn't matter. The more he could show her his kindness, the more it would soften her heart.

At least, that was his plan.

He made a quick turn and headed back toward the manor, riding faster. Suddenly, the saddle beneath him shifted, catching him off guard. At first, he wondered if he had been feeling things, but when the saddle moved again, he knew something was dreadfully wrong.

Immediately, he pulled on the reins to bring the horse to a stop, but before the animal could slow down, the saddle completely came loose. Although he tried holding on to the reins, they slipped out of his hands as he tumbled to the ground. The second he hit the dirt, he rolled, praying there was nothing that would stop him and injure him in the process.

He held his body tight until he stopped rolling. He sighed with relief and tested his arms and legs to see if there was any pain. Thankfully, everything seemed fine. Slowly, he sat up and looked around. He wasn't that far from the manor, so walking wouldn't be a problem.

As he stood, he stretched his arms and legs, and then ran his fingers through his hair. Once again, dirt covered him from head to toe, just as when he had returned to the manor yesterday and had seen Priscilla after all this time.

He glanced around to find his horse. He was certain the steed would return momentarily, even if he couldn't spot him now. But the saddle was easy to see.

Grumbling, he marched to the saddle and crouched down to study the straps. There was no reason it should have come loose, because he knew his grandmother's groom wasn't that incompetent.

Then he noticed it—a cut in the strap. Someone had purposely tampered with the leather. But why would anyone want him to fall off his horse? Then again, he was certain Priscilla wanted to hurt him.

The moment the thought popped into his head, he ushered it out. The woman may still be upset at him, but she wasn't the malicious type. She was too kind to want to cut his saddle.

He exhaled deeply and began his walk toward the manor, brushing off his clothes as he went. When he saw Priscilla next, he would be able to tell by her expression if she had been the reason he fell off his horse.

The early afternoon sun warmed him quickly. He inhaled slowly, filling his lungs with the fresh air. Sadly, being outdoors hadn't quite cleared his mind from what was happening with his inheritance. Who could be taking his money?

It occurred to him that perhaps he should make an appointment with his cousin, Trey's good friend Dominic Lawrence, Marquess of Hawthorne. Gavin had met the marquess a few times, and the one thing he learned from the encounters was that Hawthorne was a different kind of gambler. He enjoyed investing large sums of money in ventures. Thankfully, most of them paid off.

Perhaps this was how Gavin could get back some of the money that had been taken from his own coffers. Of course, he needed to find the thief before gaining any more money for fear that would mysteriously disappear, too.

As he turned the corner of the manor, women's voices rang through the air, loud with laughter. Knowing whom he would find, he quickened his step toward his grandmother's favorite spot, her flower garden.

At first, he couldn't see anyone, but as he came closer, he noticed his grandmother sitting in her rollerchair, pointing to something not far in front of her. The older woman wore pink today, which, in his opinion, made her face appear paler than normal. But this color was the woman's favorite, so he couldn't argue with her on this subject.

For a moment, he wondered why Priscilla wasn't watching her employer… until a flash of blue material caught his eye. Apparently, the lady's companion was kneeling in front of one of the multicolored daisy bushes. Since his grandmother had many bushes with this particular flower, it was difficult to see anything else.

"No, dear Priscilla. Look toward your right." His grandmother continued to point as she leaned forward.

Gavin sped up his gait, mainly for fear the younger lady

wouldn't see his grandmother slipping out of her rollerchair. If he didn't hurry, he might not catch the dowager before she fell to the ground.

Just as he reached her side, she sat back and clapped her hands. Her face lit up with a smile that nearly stretched from ear to ear. When she saw him, she hitched a breath and touched a hand to her bosom.

"Gavin? What are you doing out here?" She gasped. "And why do you look like you have been rolling in the dirt again?"

Priscilla snapped upright, holding a kitten against her chest. She was grinning until her gaze flew to his face. Locks of the young lady's black hair had come out of her fashionable bun, and one particular piece stuck on a scratch to her cheek that appeared to be bleeding. Her eyes widened as she looked him over, clearly noticing his disheveled state as her heart-shaped mouth hung open. She looked shocked, but only because he was filthy, not because he wasn't injured from the fall. Just as he suspected, she wasn't responsible for cutting his saddle.

Immediately, he dug into the pocket of his over-jacket and pulled out a handkerchief that was, thankfully, still clean. Without saying anything, he leaned toward her and dabbed the cloth against her cut. She gasped and yanked back. The kitten in her arms squirmed, and the animal's claws pulled at the material of Priscilla's day dress.

"Why did you do that?" she asked in a sharp tone.

Slowly, he straightened. *Ungrateful woman!* "Your cheek is bleeding." He showed her the tiny spot of blood on the handkerchief.

"It is nothing but something the kitten did, I assure you," she answered quickly.

"The poor kitten was frightened," Grandmother explained. "Miss Priscilla was trying to get the animal out of my flowers, and I fear it scratched her face." She cocked her head, narrowing her eyes on him. "But you still haven't explained why you are outside in the garden with us looking like *that*. Is something amiss back at the manor?"

"I needed a rest from looking over the ledgers, so I went riding." He shrugged. "Unfortunately, my saddle decided it didn't want to stay on the horse, so I fell off."

Both women gasped, but his grandmother's concern was more evident. Still, he knew Priscilla had nothing to do with his accident. It wasn't in her nature to harm someone.

"Oh, Gavin, my boy." His grandmother reached out to touch his arm. "Are you injured?"

"No, just my pride."

The dowager sighed heavily. "Thank goodness for that. Let us hope it doesn't happen again."

"I couldn't agree more." He glanced at Priscilla, who was trying to avoid looking at him. "But now I'm happy I came across the two of you, because I realize what lovely things I can find in the gardens, so I'm quite certain this won't be my last time coming out here."

Priscilla's cheeks darkened, and she threw him a glare before dropping her gaze back to the kitten. He wanted to laugh. Thankfully, his grandmother didn't mention anything about her companion's chilly attitude toward him. Then again, his grandmother was wise, and he didn't doubt she'd heard rumors about his roguish ways. He also knew the dowager, and she was quite frank when she wanted answers. He was certain that if she wondered if he had broken Priscilla's heart, she would ask. But in private, of course.

"Well, it is a very lovely day to be amongst the flowers." His grandmother smiled and looked toward her companion. "Is it not, Miss Priscilla?"

"Yes, Your Grace," Priscilla muttered.

"Gavin, perhaps you would like to join us as we continue through the gardens?" The dowager arched an eyebrow.

He wanted to laugh, but not at the old woman. It was obvious that Priscilla wasn't too happy about the invitation. Her jaw tightened and she pursed her lips. He even wondered if she tightened her hold on the kitten, but the little furball didn't cry out, so perhaps Priscilla knew how to keep her anger out of her hands. He couldn't say the same about her expression, though.

"I wouldn't want to disrupt your peaceful time in the gardens," he answered, looking back at his grandmother.

"Oh, posh! You are not disrupting us. Is he, Miss Priscilla?"

Gavin clenched his teeth and tried his hardest not to grin as he waited for the young miss's answer. She was thoroughly adorable with the wrinkles around her knees, and dirt stains not only on her dress but on her face. And her messy hair made him want to remove the pins holding the coil together at the back of her head and let the bulk tumble around her shoulders and back.

He quickly halted his wayward thoughts. He needed to stop these ideas before they grew into nothing but complicated—and improper—situations. He could *not* think of her as a desirable woman. Not when she was his grandmother's companion.

"I, um…" Priscilla cleared her throat and shifted from one foot to the other. Then her gaze jumped up to his face and her eyes widened. "I think that is a fine idea. In fact, I think His Grace should carry the kitten so that I can push your rollerchair."

Before his mind formed the polite words to refuse her request, she stepped toward him and pushed the kitten against his chest. Immediately, he grasped the ball of fur to his chest, trying to keep it from scratching him the way it had Priscilla. In the process of his getting hold of the animal, his hands brushed with hers, and warmth spread through him.

She stiffened and took a step back, lifting her chin in a stubborn stance. "Now, Your Grace, don't let the kitten get away. I don't want to crawl around near the flower bushes again tonight."

Speechless, Gavin switched his gaze between her and the animal still in his arms. What had Priscilla just done? She'd tricked him, that was what happened. And he had been foolish enough not to stop her. After all, he couldn't very well tell her *now* that he was highly allergic to cats. He didn't want her thinking him any less of a man. Then again, she probably didn't think much of him anyway.

"Make sure to pet her," the dowager told Gavin. "That will calm the little one so you don't get scratched."

Inwardly, he seethed. *Pet her?* He didn't want the animal this close to him in the first place. But now he was stuck, unless…

An idea popped into his head. Perhaps he should tell the ladies that he had an appointment with his secretary. But he would be lying, and he was certain both women would discover that soon anyway.

Sadly, the truth was the only way to get out of this situation, especially because he could feel the tightness in his head and chest from this terrible allergy. Soon, it would be difficult to swallow, and it would be followed by his face and hands swelling.

He exhaled and relaxed his shoulders, glancing at the cat. The wretched thing had actually cuddled against him. *Drat!*

"Miss Priscilla, as much as I would like to help you, I won't be able to take the kitten." He stepped closer and handed the animal back. "Unfortunately, I'm allergic to felines. In fact, now that I have touched this one, I need to excuse myself to go inside and wash my hands and face, along with change my clothes."

Her eyebrow arched as she clutched the animal. "You must be jesting. How can holding a kitten for only a few moments be that bad to make you have to wash up and change?"

He shrugged. "I cannot explain it."

"Oh, he is correct, Miss Priscilla," Grandmother said with a frown. "I now remember from when he was young. If he touched a cat, his whole face became swollen, and his eyes puffed up so much his mother had to place cold rags over them."

Thankfully, the dowager backed up his story. He was doubtful that Priscilla would've believed him otherwise.

She nodded. "Then I suppose you should go back inside and wash up. I would hate for you to become stricken with allergies."

"I thank you for understanding." He briefly touched her arm before quickly turning and hurrying back to the manor. Already, he felt his forehead growing tight and his nose becoming stuffy. Hopefully, he would make it in time. If not, he was in for one very miserable afternoon.

Chapter Four

PRISCILLA PACED THE corridor near Gavin's bedchamber. He hadn't been down for supper, and she was afraid to ask why. If his face and hands had swollen the way they had when he was younger, as the dowager had explained, Priscilla would know it was all her fault. She hated to feel guilty.

But she *was* to blame. Right after they first met, she had heard a story of him becoming so allergic he could hardly swallow. Of course, she wondered if this had been just a story for him to make women feel sorry for him, since she had never seen an allergic reaction that bad.

Although she was still vexed with him, she didn't want him to suffer from the allergy because of her. Generally, she wasn't a vicious woman. But whatever it was, Gavin just made her so upset, she wanted to get back at him however she could.

Yet this wasn't the way.

She stopped and glanced toward his door. Perhaps she should have asked the dowager about his welfare instead of coming to this part of the manor to check on him herself. This wasn't proper at all. If he were to come out of his chambers and meet her in the corridor, that would be different. At least she could offer up her apologies then. But what if he didn't come out? She couldn't wait until tomorrow, when he was better. Telling him that she was sorry would help her sleep better tonight.

She twisted her hands, wishing she wasn't so nervous. It must be done. But was it late enough in the evening that the servants wouldn't see her? The dowager had gone to bed two hours ago, so Priscilla prayed most of the servants had retired for the evening as well.

She squared her shoulders and took a deep breath for courage. She would certainly need it, because part of her wanted to turn away and hide herself in her own chambers.

As she stepped to the door, she swallowed hard, hoping to moisten her dry throat. She didn't want to come across as too nervous. But being too confident would make her appear insincere. Nor did she want to seem desperate to talk to him. Though, in reality, she was.

She hated feeling this way.

Her hand trembled when she raised it to knock, and the sound was like drums echoing in the corridor. She groaned. She was certain the whole house heard that. If they didn't, they would surely hear the hammering of her heart as it whacked against her ribs.

Although she tried to listen for footsteps on the other side of the door, the pounding in her head was too loud. But if he didn't open the door within the next few seconds, she would knock again, and harder. The servants would definitely come running then. Perhaps she should just write a note and slip it under his door.

When Gavin didn't open the door, she wondered if he was asleep and couldn't hear her. Now she wouldn't get any sleep herself, because guilt would keep her awake.

It appeared a note would have to be written before she retired for the night.

As she stepped back and started to turn, the door opened. She gasped and placed her hand to her throat.

Gavin stood in the doorway wearing nothing but a long dressing robe. But it wasn't his bare feet and bare neck that frightened her... it was his puffy eyes and swollen lips.

Her heart dropped, and she groaned. Heavens, she could have killed him.

"Priscilla, why are you here?" he snapped, slurring a bit. "I don't wish you to see me in such a state." He lowered his head and stepped back into the shadows of his room, moving out of the light from the lamp in the corridor.

The pain in her chest twisted tighter. By coming to apologize, she had embarrassed him. Still, she must say what she came to tell him and then leave quickly.

"Your Grace, please forgive me for causing you distress tonight, but more than that, I beg your forgiveness for making you touch the kitten. I didn't know…" She paused, wondering how to phrase the words without confessing that she had done it on purpose. "I didn't know your reaction to the animal would be so severe."

"Now that you know, please leave."

She nibbled on her bottom lip. Now that she had apologized, she should leave, but the maternal side of her wanted to stay to take care of him, even though the idea was ridiculous.

"Will you be all right tonight? Do you need anything from the kitchen?"

He didn't move, for which she was grateful, but she really wished he hadn't stepped into the shadows. Was he still looking at her? Was her presence still upsetting him? But as the seconds passed without him answering, she started to wonder if he had fallen asleep standing up. Or maybe the swelling had affected his voice, since he spoke to her in rough tones.

"I will be fine," he said softly. "The only thing I need is for you to return to your room and leave me alone until I have fully recovered."

She licked her dry lips. "And when will that be, Your Grace?"

He groaned and rubbed his forehead. It appeared his fingers were slightly swollen as well. Could her guilt become any worse?

"I will be back to my normal, cheerful self by tomorrow, I assure you."

She nodded, trying to relax. "Before I leave, will you please accept my apology?"

"Not to worry yourself, Priscilla. You have done nothing wrong."

Unfortunately, she had. But perhaps this wasn't the time to tell him the truth. She would wait until he was improved and could handle the news better. Maybe he would be so put out with her that he would leave the manor and not want to return.

"Then I bid you good night," she said.

As she turned to leave, she felt slightly better, but she feared sleep would still not come as quickly as she wanted.

"Wait," he called out.

She swung back around and faced him. He had stepped more into the light, but not enough. "What is it?"

"Although I'm reluctant to ask, I fear I must."

"Tell me what you need."

"I wasn't hungry until you mentioned food. Will you get me something from the icebox?"

Her heart lightened slightly at knowing he was allowing her to help him, even in the smallest measurement. "Of course, Your Grace. Whatever you want."

"Bread and cheese will be fine."

"Then I shall return momentarily."

This time when she walked down the corridor, her steps were faster. Maybe she would feel better now that she could care for him a little. And thankfully, she didn't have to enter his bedchamber to do it.

―――― ⚜ ――――

GAVIN SAT ON his cushioned chair, watching the opened door to his room. Although his face hurt and his head felt like it would explode soon, he was actually quite stunned at his visitor. It pleased him to think she had gone against Society's rules and come to his chambers just to apologize. He knew it would take some coaxing to get her to forgive him for breaking her heart, but what she'd done tonight was something he never expected.

She had obviously glimpsed his ugly, swollen face, because he noticed her slight cringe. However, she hadn't run away screaming, and that was a good sign. But he hadn't thought she would offer to get him something to eat. He was relieved his pride—or was it embarrassment?—hadn't stopped him from allowing her to assist in his recovery.

It shamed him to have her see him in this condition. As a child, his governess was the one to take care of him when he had become allergic, but as an adult, he hid away in his room until the swelling went down, suffering through the pain alone. Now, knowing Priscilla would return with his food, he welcomed the company for the first time. Of course, he would stay in the shadows as much as he could, but leave a single candle burning near the door, and the low-burning fire in the hearth on the other side of the room, so at least she would see his outline when she entered the room.

As the grandfather clock in the corridor ticked the minutes away, Gavin wondered what was taking so long. Preparing a plate of bread and cheese was not that difficult to do. Although he had been waited on most of his life, he could get his own food from the kitchen. So why couldn't Priscilla? Unless she had been stopped by a servant and was fearful of their being aware of *why* she was making him a plate.

Gavin drummed his fingers on the armrest of the chair. He studied his hand through the shadows, but could tell the swelling had gone down quite a bit. However, his face still felt like an oversized watermelon.

His stomach grumbled. He hadn't wanted to eat, mainly because it was difficult to swallow, but now he was eager for nutrition. His body needed the satisfaction that only food could provide. If only she would get here…

Gavin stood and slowly moved toward the door, listening for

her footsteps, but the hall remained quiet. He frowned. Where was she? Perhaps it was late enough that he could venture downstairs to the kitchen and find his own food. It was obvious that she had decided against helping him.

He pulled the dressing robe around his body and tightened the sash around his waist. If his grandmother ever found out her companion had seen him in this state of undress, Priscilla would lose her employment for sure. The dowager duchess was a stickler for the rules, unlike her grandson, who didn't care if he went downstairs looking this way.

As he reached the stairs, he heard the gentle tap of someone's shoe coming up. Realizing it must be Priscilla, he hurried back into his room and returned to his cushioned chair. His heartbeat raced, and he took deep breaths to calm himself. He wasn't sure if he was more excited over the food or seeing Priscilla again.

He watched her as she came toward his room, and then slowed considerably as she reached his open door. In her hands was a tray of food and a teacup. He could hardly see her expression, but it was easy to see her hesitation.

"Um, Your Grace?" she asked in a quiet voice.

"I'm here."

She held up the tray. "I have this for you."

"Can you bring it in and put it on the table by the candle?"

Her eyes widened. "Oh, no. That wouldn't be proper."

Gavin tried not to grin. "I know it is not proper, but I cannot move very well." That wasn't exactly a lie. His ankles were slightly swollen.

She didn't say anything, but shifted back and forth from one leg to the other. She glanced down the corridor and then quickly stepped into his room and hurried to the table, where she placed the tray.

"I brought what you requested," she said. "Plus, I made you some tea with a touch of honey and a crushed butterbar leaf." She pointed to a smaller object on the tray. "I also found the root of a pineapple that your grandmother had for breakfast, and also a peppermint leaf."

Confusion filled him and he shook his head. He had no idea what a butterbar leaf was. "Why did you bring those for me?"

"Well, you see, the butterbar leaf will help the rashes on your skin due to allergies. The root of a pineapple, along with the peppermint leaf, will help with the swelling."

Was he hearing her correctly? She actually knew how to help his allergies when the family physician and even his governess had no knowledge of how to cure him?

"How do you know these things?"

A smile graced her lovely face. "Because my mother's family were healers. All my sisters learned from our mother before she passed away."

"Your mother was a physician?"

"No, not really. But she knew what plants to use that helped maladies. That is why I knew what to bring for you."

His heart softened. "That is very thoughtful of you, Priscilla."

"All you have to do is drink the tea, and use the peppermint leaf and butterbar on your skin, and it will take the pain, itching, and swelling away."

He chuckled. "It sounds so simple."

"It really is. The only thing complicated about it was grinding up butterbar leaves to add to the tea. I am grateful your grandmother's cook had the peppermint and honey in her spice rack."

"As am I." He shifted in his chair to stand, but really didn't want her to see more of him than necessary. As much as he wanted to keep her in his room, it was best that she leave. "I thank you again, Priscilla. I believe I can handle things from this point forward."

She nodded. "I pray you feel better tomorrow."

"As do I."

As he watched her turn to leave, but stop at the doorway again to look up and down the corridor before she hurried out, he couldn't stop the smile from stretching across his swollen face. Perhaps he could hope she would be civil to him after this, and within time, maybe forgive him for being a mule's back end? It would be a pleasure to become her friend.

Chapter Five

"I DON'T UNDERSTAND any of this," Gavin grumbled, smacking his fist on the desk.

His secretary, Jacob McGuire, frowned. "Indeed, Your Grace. These books are very confusing. I wish your father's secretary had kept better track of where the funds were going, and especially what was coming in."

Thankfully, Gavin's allergies had miraculously disappeared, and this morning he showed no signs of being disfigured for most of yesterday. However, his current headache was because he and his secretary were going over the books more closely, trying to find something that might point them in the direction of the missing money.

"Be honest with me, McGuire. Do you think we will ever discover who is stealing my money?"

The man in his mid-forties shrugged and scratched his balding head. "My opinion is that if we keep digging and trying to find some of your father's other papers, we might just find the connection."

Gavin groaned and leaned his elbows on the desk, resting his head in his hands. How many times did he have to curse his dead father? Why had the man done this to his only son? Gavin vowed that if *he* ever married and sired children, he would never leave them with this kind of struggle.

"I cannot think anymore today, unfortunately." Gavin sighed and sat up straighter. "Let us give this matter a rest for a few days, and during that time, I shall have some of the servants search through the manor and see what they can find."

"What about the other estates your father owned?" Jacob asked.

"My father only conducted business here, and that was because he was following *his* father's example. However, it wouldn't hurt to send some of the servants to those estates to search as well. I will place them on the block to sell soon, so perhaps now is the best time to try to find missing ledgers."

"You are correct, Your Grace."

Gavin stood, and his secretary rose from his chair as well. "I do appreciate your assistance with this matter, McGuire. I beg your secrecy, at least for now. I don't need my grandmother worried needlessly, or for the servants to think we can't afford to pay them and start looking for other employment."

"Of course, Your Grace. As always, I kept my client's issues to myself."

"You are a good man, and a wonderful friend."

"As are you." Jacob bowed and left the room.

Gavin stretched his arms above his head to release the kinks in his shoulders and back. He should get out of this stuffy office and stretch his legs as well. If only he could occupy his mind with something else, because trying to find the missing money was too stressful.

He stepped out into the hall. First things first—he needed to have Martin, the butler, send a missive to his other estates, and have the servants still in residence search through the manors for any hidden ledgers or books created by his father. Once their work was finished, he would, sadly, need to sell his lands.

Angrily he marched toward the other end of the manor, fisting his hands and cursing his father once again. He couldn't help but think of his Worthington cousins who held titles. They were all productive and didn't have to worry about people stealing from their coffers. Perhaps he should contact his cousin Trevor Worthington, Duke of Kenbridge. There was a man who could handle several estates on his own, even though he was recently widowed.

A heavenly scent drifted all around him, and his stomach grumbled. It smelled like the cooks were busy making pastries. Of course, that only meant that the dowager duchess was having an afternoon social. If not now, then soon.

He turned down another corridor, heading for the parlor where his grandmother usually held her small gatherings. The closer he came, the more he heard women's voices. The few times he had stayed at the manor, the old woman invited him to "drop in" to see her during her get-togethers. Of course, it didn't take him long to realize she had invited young women merely to make introductions on the chance that he might become interested in one of them.

Gavin figured this time would be no different. After all, he was now living at the manor, and once again, she was having a party.

As he neared, he slowed his steps as he heard the women's chatter inside the room. It sounded like they were aiming their grievances at some poor chap, even though Gavin hadn't caught a name as of yet.

"He is as wicked as they come," a younger woman spouted irritably. "The man had the audacity to try to pay off my chaperone so that she would leave me alone with him."

Gasps ricocheted around the room. Gavin grinned. Why hadn't *he* thought of doing that in his roguish years? Why, it was pure genius. But at least he knew they weren't discussing his exploits. Then again, his grandmother wouldn't allow any such talk about her grandson in front of company.

"Then your chaperone is to be commended for not giving in and taking the money," the dowager said in a strong voice. "But I must admit, there are worse men out there than that. You young ladies need to remember not to feel temptation to these types of men. Their charms will only ruin your good name, and you will never marry well once that happens. Not long after I married, my sister fell prey to a seducer, and her life has been miserable ever since."

Gavin nodded. Aunt Mildred was the pitiful relative that the family never wanted to talk about, only because she fell in love with the wrong man, a man who could not return her feelings and wouldn't do the right thing and marry her after taking her maidenhood.

Gavin now wished *he* hadn't been that kind of man. At the time, he never cared about anyone but himself. Hopefully, he had grown since becoming a duke. If not, he would certainly have to work on it.

He stopped at the door but stayed against the wall, not wanting to be seen just yet. Perhaps making his presence known during this particular conversation wasn't a good idea, especially because he had probably seduced—or attempted seduction—with some of the young misses having afternoon tea with his grandmother. He knew at least one of them. Thankfully, Priscilla would keep that secret until her last breath.

"Your Grace, your wisdom is so very much appreciated, and I'm certain these young ladies would be wise to follow your example."

The voice came from a middle-aged woman, but she didn't sound familiar to Gavin. He was certain he hadn't met all of his grandmother's friends, even though she'd tried to make the introductions. Her matchmaking skills were quite obvious, whether she knew it or not.

"How kind of you to say, Lady Browning," the dowager duchess said confidently. "I certainly want to share my knowledge in hopes of helping some young lady."

Gavin bit his lip to keep from laughing. If these ladies only knew what kind of troublemaker his grandmother had been in her younger years, they would leave the party with burned ears and warped minds. But he wouldn't tell. However, he was growing rather bored of eavesdropping, and although he didn't want to go in and have his grandmother introduce him to the maidens who were looking for a husband, he may as well get it over and done with.

He moved away from the wall and walked inside. The women were sitting in a large circle, sipping their tea and eating pastries. He wouldn't mind eating the few pastries still left on the cart, but he would refrain. Of course, once he left, the kitchen would be his next stop.

"Good afternoon, ladies," he greeted them loudly, getting their attention.

Almost in unison, the women's heads turned toward him, and the eyes of the young misses grew wide as they straightened in their chairs. But once his attention landed on one certain woman, he didn't want to look any further.

Priscilla was lovely today in her cream and peach silk day dress. The see-through short sleeves and square bodice enhanced her slender figure. Her black hair was fashioned in a loose coil, leaving wisps of curls around her ears and along her neck. Although he hadn't studied the other women in the room, he could honestly admit he had never seen a more beautiful woman.

"Oh, goodness." The dowager's voice lifted with excitement. "You have come."

It was difficult, but he tore his gaze from Priscilla and focused on the hostess as he walked to her chair. He leaned down and kissed her cheek. "Of course, Grandmother. After all, you invited me, or have you forgotten?"

She laughed and patted his cheek. "I have invited you many times, but it is a rare occasion when you actually come."

"Well, I thought I would take a break from my duties and visit for a moment with you and your friends." He moved his gaze back to Priscilla. Although she didn't look on him with bashful eyes, like some of the other young misses were doing, at least her attention was on him and not her lap.

"Splendid." The dowager squeezed his arm. "Then I pray you

will take a moment and allow me to introduce you to some of my guests."

"But of course." He smiled, not wanting the introduction—but he would try to be patient regardless.

"You remember Lady Caldwell, and this is her daughter Miss Beatrice."

As his grandmother introduced each woman, he nodded or gave them a polite greeting. Yet he couldn't stop his gaze from jumping back toward Priscilla from time to time. How could he help himself, especially after the kindness she'd shown him last night, when she had reason to loathe his very presence?

"I'm not sure if you remember," his grandmother continued, "but this is Lady Burns, who was friends with your parents, and her daughter, Miss Georgina."

Gavin briefly glanced at the daughter, giving her a nod, but then something caught his interest, making him want to look at her longer. Her wavy, dark brown hair was the same color as his, but it was her memorable green eyes that made his mind stall. His father also had those eyes and that hair, which were passed down to Gavin. But it was more than that which made him think he was looking at someone familiar. Her face structure was very much like his father's, long nose, high cheekbones, and small ears—something Gavin had not gotten from his father.

And the girl's name was Georgina. How odd, since his father's name had been George. Strange, but the young woman stared at him as though challenging him.

Gavin's stomach twisted, and his gaze jumped back to the young woman's mother. Another thing he found odd was that Lady Burns wasn't meeting his eyes, and her cheeks grew pinker by the second.

Inwardly, he groaned. Did his father really think he could hide it from the family? Gavin was surprised his grandmother hadn't noticed the resemblance between him and the girl. And did his mother know about her husband's infidelity before she passed on?

"And this is Mrs. Smythe, visiting from London," his grandmother continued.

He tried not to show his irritation as he finished greeting the other women in the circle, but at this moment, he didn't want to be here. Hadn't his father ruined his son's life enough?

When he heard Priscilla's name, he snapped out of his anger and stared at her beauty once again. Just seeing her look at him with her pretty blue eyes softened his heart.

"It is good to see you again, Your Grace," she said, curtsying. "I trust you are well?"

"Indeed, I am. And how are you faring?"

She nodded. "It has been a wonderful day, thank you."

"I'm so happy to hear that."

"Gavin, my boy," his grandmother said, forgetting to use his title in front of her guests, "would you stay and take some tea and pastries with us?"

He looked down at her. "Thank you for the offer, but no. I need to be getting back to the ledgers."

Although he didn't want to get back to them, he didn't know what other excuse to give her. Gavin didn't know if Lady Burns had told her daughter who sired her, but it was plain to him who the girl's father was, and at this moment, he didn't want to see her or his father's former mistress.

He turned to the group of ladies and nodded. "I shall leave you to return to your socializing."

As he left, he heard their chimes of goodbyes. He tried not to appear as though he was in a hurry, but truly, he was. He wished he knew whom to trust to talk with about his father's other offspring, and the only people he could think of were his cousins. However, that would mean meeting them at the gaming tables, and since he didn't have money to throw away, he didn't dare go there.

He strode toward the nearest exit. Riding around the estate would soothe him. It always had. But with this current shock to his system, would he ever recover?

PRISCILLA WAS GRATEFUL to be away from the manor as she rode the mare that her employer had given permission to take. She'd enjoyed the guests the Dowager Duchess of Englewood had at her party, even if Priscilla noticed the condescending stares some of the older women had tossed her way. It was obvious that she had been the subject of their gossip lately. Of course, it didn't help when her father had tried pushing his daughters to marry any wealthy man, no matter what was needed to make it happen.

Thankfully, her sister Bridget had married well, but Priscilla would never find that kind of happiness. If only people didn't have to gossip about her family.

She had been able to handle the ladies' uppity manners—until Gavin had entered the room. She was relieved to see him looking back to normal, and she would love to talk to him in private about the remedies she had given him, but when she saw the way he looked at Miss Georgina, Priscilla was hit by a feeling she hadn't experienced in quite a while.

Why she felt any kind of jealousy, she wished she knew. Gavin was certainly not worth feeling that way about. Yet the way he'd studied Miss Georgina had Priscilla wishing he would look at her that way.

It shouldn't matter to her whom he decided to seduce, as long as it wasn't her.

She stopped the horse and glanced around the area. She couldn't remember the exact places within the perimeter of the lands, but she thought the neighbor's land was close by. Even if she had broken a few rules in her life—being in Gavin's room last night was one of those times—she generally followed the straight and narrow, so trespassing wasn't something she wanted to do.

Priscilla guided the animal toward a stream, but before she reached the water, a strong gust of wind knocked against her. She looked up and noticed gray clouds gathering quickly.

She frowned. Just her luck that it would rain when she wanted to go riding. But then, she could go tomorrow. For the rest of the afternoon while the dowager napped, Priscilla would stay in her room and read the book she had borrowed from the library this morning.

She pulled the reins, trying to move the horse around to head back toward the manor. Another gust of wind pushed against her, stronger this time. The wind rattled the branches in the trees and startled her horse. Since she knew how to calm the horse, she wasn't worried… until the animal started bucking wildly as if afraid of something.

Panicked, she leaned forward, tightening her hold on the reins and trying to stay on the sidesaddle without falling off. That was when she saw the reason for the horse's distress. *A snake!*

If she didn't get the horse away from the reptile quickly, she would find herself on the ground while the animal ran away.

That was unacceptable. She hadn't been thrown from a horse since she was ten years old, and she didn't plan on ending that record today.

Chapter Six

GAVIN TROTTED HIS horse near a stream until he felt the first drop of rain. He was nearly home and knew the shower wouldn't ruin his afternoon ride. In fact, he welcomed the moisture, since both he and his steed were hot from riding for two hours.

He whipped his riding crop across some bushes to clear the way as he peered toward the neighboring land. Lord Rothwell didn't take care of his estate very well, and several times throughout the years, Gavin's father would complain to the neighboring lord about certain reptiles crossing the border. Nothing was ever done about it, of course, but it had made Gavin's father feel better criticizing the other nobleman. Then again, the former duke usually had something negative to say about most people.

Just as he turned the animal back toward the path, Gavin heard the panicked neigh of another horse, followed quickly by a woman's cry. Maneuvering the animal around, he searched through the trees and shrubbery, trying to locate the source of the distress. Within seconds, one of his grandmother's horses ran past him—minus a rider.

Gavin cursed under his breath and urged his horse in the direction from where the frantic animal had come. The blue from a woman's riding habit on the ground amongst the tall weeds on the edge of Lord Rothwell's land captured his attention. Gavin kicked the horse's flanks and rode faster, stopping only when he reached the fallen woman.

As he jumped off the animal, he recognized her. Priscilla lay curled up, holding her ankle and rocking back and forth. Her red face was scrunched in pain. When she saw him, she released a sob.

"Cilla, what's happened?" He knelt by her side, reaching for her foot.

"A snake spooked my mare, and I was tossed to the ground." Gingerly, she touched her ankle and flinched. "I hadn't wanted to cross to Lord Rothwell's land, but I couldn't stop the horse. I think I sprained my ankle when I landed."

"Put your arms around my neck and let me lift you. I will take you back to the house." He glanced around them. "Is my grandmother out here as well?"

"No, she is taking a nap, but I assure you, she gave me permission to ride."

"I'm not questioning that in the least. I'm grateful I don't have two women to assist when there is only one horse."

"Your grandmother wouldn't have been thrown from her horse, I'm sure."

He smiled. "Although she is a great horsewoman, I doubt she would have remained on her mare if a snake upset the animal as it did yours."

Another drop of rain landed on his cheek. Inwardly, he growled. They needed to hurry before they became drenched from the storm. He didn't care about himself, but he couldn't have Priscilla sick from pneumonia, especially if she suffered from a sprained ankle as well.

Priscilla lifted her arms hesitantly, as though she were afraid to touch him. Not having the patience for this, he helped her wrap her arms around his neck before gently lifting her. As he stood, he whistled for his horse. Thankfully, he had trained the animal to listen for his voice and respond immediately.

Gavin realized, as he placed Priscilla on the saddle, that her hair lay in disarray around her shoulders. Even her bonnet was missing. But he couldn't worry about that now. The bonnet wouldn't stop her head from getting wet anyway.

She shifted on the saddle, holding on to the horn. He mounted behind her but found there wasn't enough room. Although she wouldn't like it, there was only one thing for him to do. He lifted her once again, and she cried out, grasping his arms.

"What are you doing?" she asked in a panicked voice.

"I'm setting you on my lap."

"Whatever for?"

He tilted his head, gazing into her confused, yet lovely, face. "To make the ride more comfortable. We will need to ride fast in order to reach home before the rain drowns us both."

Her jaw tightened and she nodded. He wanted to laugh at her reaction, but there wasn't time for teasing. The sooner they returned home, the better.

Gavin circled an arm around her waist to keep her in place as he guided the horse toward the manor. Within minutes, water fell from the clouds heavier and faster than before. Priscilla turned her face toward his chest. Perhaps this wasn't the right time to find pleasure in the moment, but he enjoyed that she wanted his protection.

He was probably only fifteen minutes from the house, but certainly, they would both be drenched. His grandmother would reprimand him for being careless when it came to his health, and the health of her companion. He was certain he would never hear the end of it from the old lady.

Making a quick decision, he turned the horse toward the woodsman's cottage, which should be empty this early in the spring. There should be firewood, and with any luck, the place would be stocked with some necessities while he and Priscilla were sheltered from the storm.

Minutes later, he reached the cottage and quickly dismounted. This time when he reached for her, he didn't have to encourage her to hold on to his neck. Her arms were already outstretched and waiting for his assistance.

He hastened his step as he carried her to the cottage. Thankfully, the door was unlocked, and he was able to walk inside without any hindrance. Without a word, he placed her on the sofa near the hearth, and then quickly hurried back outside to tie his horse under the lean-to on the other end of the structure.

By the time he entered the cottage again, his hair was dripping wet, as well as his coat. Thankfully, though, he wasn't drenched all the way through.

Priscilla sat near the hearth, adding the kindling to start a fire. He smiled. She must have read his mind.

As he knelt beside her, he took the piece of wood out of her hands. "I can do this now."

She scowled. "And so can I. Believe it not, Your Grace, I'm not an invalid."

Her snappy attitude surprised him, but he figured it was due to the pain in her ankle. "I never thought you were."

"And I will have you know that for years my family was without servants, and every night my sister and I traded off building a fire in the hearth in our bedroom."

Now *that* he hadn't known. He had heard rumors about her poor family, but Gavin had no idea that her life had been reduced so drastically.

"Forgive me, then." He sighed and handed her the piece of wood. "If you would like to start the fire, I shall look for some blankets."

Her face relaxed slightly, and she nodded, taking the wood and placing it in the hearth.

He stood and brushed his hands down his trousers. They were damp, but not overly so. However, if they didn't start a fire soon, both of them would be chilled to the bone. The temperature outside had plummeted once the rain came.

It only took him about five minutes to find two blankets before he returned to the main room. He tried not to act shocked when he noticed the blazing fire in the hearth. Priscilla sat on the floor next to the fire as she struggled with removing her boot. Her pained expression let him know her ankle was still hurting.

Once again, he knelt by her side, handing her a blanket. "Would you like some help with your boot?"

Her eyes widened and her cheeks grew red. "No, I'm fine."

He grumbled under his breath, "You are *not* fine, Cilla. I can see the pain on your face. Now, I suggest allowing me to help you, or you will see how stubborn *I* can be, because I will do it myself."

Ignoring her argument, he gently lifted her foot to his lap and continued to unlace the heeled boot. She slapped his hands, but he didn't stop. Finally, she sighed and leaned back, letting him remove it. As he slid it off her foot, she grimaced and released a slight moan.

Immediately, he could see her ankle was swollen through her damp stockings. He lifted his gaze to hers. She watched him through hooded eyes.

"We should remove your wet stockings."

She shook her head. "I appreciate your concern, but I think I will leave them on."

Stubborn woman! "I understand the situation we are in is improper, but will you think about this for a moment? If you leave your wet clothes on, you will catch a chill that could eventually turn into pneumonia. Then, pray, how are you going to be my grandmother's companion if you are deathly ill?"

Slowly, awareness dawned on her face, and she exhaled deeply. "Fine, but you will *not* help."

He shrugged and moved away as she spread the blanket around her legs. He stepped toward the window, almost grateful that she wouldn't let him help. Touching her bare leg all the way above her knee just to untie the ribbon holding her stocking was too personal. Even being alone with her would cause a scandal, but they really had no other choice as the storm pelted buckets of water from the gray sky. He would do all he could not to let the rumor spread that they were in the cottage without proper chaperoning.

From the looks of it, the storm wasn't going to let up for a while. Could he possibly carry on a civil conversation with her? But perhaps being forced to stay together in the cottage was a good thing. Now they might be able to talk about the past and clear the air between them. And if he was fortunate, she would realize he was a different man now.

He peeked over his shoulder to where she still sat in front of the fire. She had removed both stockings and draped them over a wooden chair next to the fire. As she stared at the flames licking the wall of the hearth while smoke drifted upward, she tightened the blanket wrapped around her. She made certain not to give him a glimpse of her arms or legs, just her head and neck.

Gavin moved back to her side and stopped. "Would you like me to help you to the sofa? I'm sure it will be more comfortable. Not only that, but we should also prop your foot up so that the swelling goes down."

She glanced at him with steely blue eyes. "I don't need your help, Your Grace."

She shifted on the ground until she was on her knees, but he could see how she struggled to crawl. The confounded woman would drive him crazy, he was certain of it. Why was she so obstinate? He had never met a more hardheaded woman in his life.

He clenched his jaw to stop from saying anything and took her in his arms. She gasped and glared at him, but he carried her to the sofa anyway, setting her down close to the edge so that she could prop her foot up on the armrest.

He stood above her, folding his arms across his chest. "Cilla, I must confess how tired I am of your ungrateful attitude. Let me point out that if I hadn't found you and brought you here, you would still be sitting in the middle of nowhere with a bruised ankle with no shelter from the storm."

She rolled her eyes and moved her leg to the armrest of the

sofa before adjusting the blanket on her again so he couldn't see the bare limb. "Don't you think I'm aware of that? Do you know how frustrating that is for me?"

"Frustrating?"

"Yes." She swung her gaze toward him. "I hate feeling helpless, especially around you."

"Why?"

"You really do not know?"

Gavin didn't appreciate it when people looked at him as if he was daft, which was the exact way Priscilla was staring at him. Of course he knew; he had just hoped that after all this time, she would have forgiven him—or at least forgotten about it.

Grumbling, he moved to the nearest cushioned chair and plopped down. "Would it help if I apologize for being a horse's back end the last time we were together?"

She made a sound that was close to a laugh. "It might help if I knew you sincerely meant your apology. But cads like yourself are never sorry for breaking a woman's heart or ruining her reputation."

His breath caught in his throat. "I... Did I... *ruin* your reputation? Is that why you haven't wed?"

"Of course not. We never did anything that could be misconstrued as any sort of an affair. But the point is, I'm sure you have ruined other women's reputations. And if we hadn't been interrupted those few times, I'm sure I would have been one of those ladies who were shunned from Society."

He frowned, knowing she was correct. He had tried to seduce her on several occasions, but when things hadn't worked out, he gave up and moved on. "Then I sincerely apologize for hurting you. I hadn't realized that you might have liked me more than I had realized."

"Well, I was foolish, and the incident taught me not to give away my heart so freely."

"Will you forgive me, then?"

She shrugged as her attention dropped to the blanket again.

She smoothed her hand over the material. "I'll consider it."

"That is all I ask for now," he said truthfully, hoping she might eventually forgive him.

As he studied her, he could see the deep sadness written on her face. His gut twisted. He knew he was the one who had done that. Why hadn't he realized that the art of seduction might harm someone? All he had cared about was his own pleasure.

He prayed he never turned back into that selfish man. But apparently, he needed to somehow show her that he wasn't the man he had been eighteen months ago. But the question was, would she ever see him for anything other than a despicable cad?

Silence passed between them, and the only sound was the popping of the wood as it burned. There was no better time than the present to show her how he had changed. At least, he hoped she would see that.

He cleared his throat. "I never got the chance to thank you for helping me last night. The tea and the peppermint leaf worked wonders with my allergies."

Priscilla met his gaze again, and she didn't appear to be as sad as a moment ago. "I noticed when you came into the parlor earlier today that you didn't look sick at all."

He nodded. "My swelling went down not long after you left, and I was able to breathe better. I slept like a babe, in fact."

She smiled. "That is good to know."

"I have to commend you again for having that skill and knowledge. You are the first person who ever took the time to find something that would cure me of the allergy. Usually, I'm in bed for days suffering through the malady." He gave her a smile. "I hope you don't mind me telling you, but last night, you were my rescuer."

Her cheeks flamed red, and she quickly turned her head to look toward the hearth. "You shouldn't say such things, Your Grace."

"Then you would have me lie?"

She snuck a peek at him. "No, of course not. But speaking

your mind is quite bold."

He shrugged. "I'm not certain how well you know me, but being bold is something that comes naturally. Besides, how else can I let you know how very much I appreciated your help last night?"

"Most men would just say *thank you*."

He chuckled. "I'm not like most men, Cilla."

Gavin noticed a grin sneaking across her mouth, but she turned her face away from him again.

"And most men would ask a lady's permission to be so casual with her name before speaking it."

"Beg your pardon, then." He paused. "Miss Priscilla, can I have your permission to say your name using my own form of endearment?"

She looked at him again, and this time it didn't appear at all as if she was embarrassed. He would say she was still *slightly* annoyed.

"Form of endearment? Really, Your Grace. That is taking things a little too far."

He held up his hands in surrender. "But because of our past, calling you Priscilla just will not do."

"Nobody has ever called me Cilla. My sisters called me Prissy."

Gavin shook his head. "You are definitely not a Prissy. That name is too girlish, if you ask me. But you are indeed a woman full grown, and you need a more desirous name—like Cilla."

She rolled her eyes and laughed. "You cannot help it, can you?"

"What are you referring to?"

"Your adorable charm, of course." She flipped her hand in the air. "You do it with such flair, I don't know if you are being sarcastic or sincere."

His heart lightened as a grin stretched the corners of his mouth. "You think I'm adorable?"

"I didn't say that," she answered quickly.

"You most certainly did." He laughed, loving that her cheeks were flaming with color again.

"Well, I didn't mean it like you think I did. It was an observation, not flattery."

"Whatever you say, Cilla."

She glared, but he could tell she was being playful. He enjoyed that side of her.

"Your Grace, you are impossible."

He nodded. "That I am, but I would like you to call me Gavin. I recall a time when you said my name with such tenderness in your voice."

Her playful expression vanished, and she appeared panicked. "I fear I cannot. I don't want to become that personal with you."

His hopes dropped. "I understand, but I hope you know that we can be friends, and as such, you can call me Gavin."

"I shall keep that in mind, Your Grace."

Gavin stood, moved to the hearth, and tossed another log onto the fire. He took the poker and moved the broken log and ashes. When he straightened, he walked to the window and peered outside. The rain continued to fall in buckets.

Although he was not in any hurry to return to the manor, he was certain his grandmother would be worried. He didn't want to lie to her, yet if he mentioned that he and Priscilla were in the woodsman's cottage during the storm, the dowager might guilt him into doing the "right thing" and marrying Priscilla.

He still didn't want a wife. Not now, when there was so much turmoil with the estate and finding the stolen money. No matter what, he needed to come up with a good excuse to tell his grandmother so that he could get out of marriage—and not ruin Priscilla's name in the process.

Chapter Seven

Priscilla stared at the fire that was getting smaller and smaller by the second. They were out of wood, and yet the rain still poured from the heavens. The pain in her ankle had lessened as well as the swelling, but she still kept it propped on the edge of the sofa. She didn't know the exact time, but she was getting hungry. Gavin had wandered through the cottage a few times, and from the sounds of his grumbling, he hadn't found any food.

He stood by the rain-streaked window, staring outside. Even if he didn't say it, she knew he was worried about their situation because he kept glancing at the fire as it slowly dwindled. When he glanced at it again, he sighed and turned toward her.

"How does your ankle feel?"

She shrugged. "It is not throbbing as badly as it was earlier, but then, I haven't placed my weight on it."

He motioned toward the window. "The rain doesn't look like it is stopping anytime soon. I fear we will soon need to head back to the house regardless of the storm. We have no choice. There is no food, and no more firewood."

"Yes, I know."

He walked to the sofa and crouched down to her level, staring into her eyes. Up this close, she had forgotten how green his eyes were, and how she had loved looking into them before. He had eyes that could melt her quicker than ice on a hot day.

"Cilla, will you be able to make the ride with me back to the house? I guarantee we will be soaked clear through, but at least we will be home to change and eat."

Nodding, she turned on the sofa, slowly moving her foot to the floor. "Let me put my stockings and boots back on first."

He walked to the wooden chair by the fire and grabbed her stockings and boots, bringing them back to her. "Would you like me to help you?"

She arched an eyebrow. "Have we not already had this conversation?"

He chuckled. "Yes, but I was hoping your answer would be different this time."

Priscilla knew that this was part of his charm. She just had to get used to it, even if she constantly reminded him that although he might not be a true *gentleman*, she was still a lady. "I'm sorry, but I must stick to my original answer."

He grinned and moved away. "Then while you finish dressing, I shall venture outside and get the horse ready. I shall also give you enough time to pull your stockings and boots on before coming to get you."

"I appreciate your thoughtfulness, Your Grace."

Once he left, she quickly pulled up her gown, which was thankfully mostly dry now, and yanked on her stockings, taking care not to bump against her ankle too much. When she tried to wiggle her foot, the sprain was still quite sore, but she still attempted to slide her foot into her boot. Pain shot up her leg, making her cry out. Letting her injured leg rest, she slid her other foot into her boot and laced it up.

Taking deep breaths, she willed herself to fight against the pain. Her boot must go on no matter what. She bit down hard and tried again, being more careful this time as she inched the boot up over her toes, but the moment it touched her ankle, the fierce pain returned.

Frustrated, she sobbed and closed her eyes. There was no

way around it. She would have to ride back to the manor without a boot.

Just then the door opened, and she looked up at Gavin as he entered. He grumbled and swiped the water off his head and face. He closed the door with more force than she thought he should have. Something must be dreadfully wrong.

When he looked at her, she could read it in his expression. Indeed, something wasn't right.

"The horse has run off," he snapped.

Groaning, she closed her eyes and rubbed her forehead. "Without the animal we will have to walk, which means you need to go without me."

"No." He knelt on one knee in front of her. "I'm not going to leave you here."

She found it odd how concerned he was about her welfare. His expression showed the helplessness he felt. It pleased her to know he was actually thinking about her instead of himself at a time like this. Then again, he had thought about her a lot since he found her on the ground after the mare had run away.

"If we can't ride your horse, and we can't stay here, are you going to carry me in the rain all the way back to the house?"

Gavin shrugged. "If I have to."

She tried not to let his selfless gesture soften her heart. "I can't let you do that, Your Grace. We will both catch our deaths from the cold, most definitely. Besides that, if you are as hungry as I am, I know you won't have the strength to carry me all that way."

Raking his fingers through his hair, he blew out a heavy breath. "There has got to be some food in this place." He turned his head and peered toward the door leading into the kitchen.

Priscilla's mind scrambled to remember what it had been like those few months her family scraped for food. She touched his arm until he looked at her. "Gavin? Do you think there is a garden close by? I know it is early spring, but I wonder if there are any vegetables that survived the winter."

His eyes widened and he smiled. "You said my name."

Inwardly, she groaned. Indeed, she had, but she hadn't meant to. *How embarrassing!* "Yes, well… I have decided that you are correct. We are friends, and as such, I shall call you by your given name, but only when we are alone."

She quickly bit her bottom lip, praying he didn't take that as an invitation for them to be alone more often. If he did, she would set him straight in a heartbeat.

"I'm glad we are friends. And I'm also happy that your mind is working better than mine. I will indeed go back outside and search for a garden. If memory serves, I believe there was one not long ago." He took her hand and gently rubbed her fingers. "Pray that I find something soon."

"I shall."

Once he was gone, a strange coolness seeped through her body. She wished her body hadn't heated when he rubbed her fingers, because now she felt the emptiness filling her as he left. Shivering, she wrapped the blanket tighter around her shoulders. Whatever it took, she must not let him touch her so tenderly again. She couldn't afford another heartbreak. Besides, he'd shown interest in Georgina Burns, and Priscilla would not stand in their way.

Slowly, she rose to her feet, trying to add pressure to her sore ankle. Now that she knew she had to walk on it no matter how much it hurt, she clenched her teeth and struggled through the pain as she hobbled into the kitchen.

Two large cooking stoves took up most of the small space, and a wall covered with hanging pots and pans decorated the far side. She limped along the counters, peeking in every drawer and every space that might have stored some food, but she found nothing. She opened the two stoves, and as luck would have it, there were a few half-burned logs in there. At least they could stay warm for a little while longer, even if they were starving.

Priscilla carefully pulled out the logs, carried them back into the front room, and knelt in front of the hearth. The flames grew once the logs were inside, but she knew it wouldn't take long before the fire dwindled again.

Brushing her charcoaled hands on her dress, she struggled to stand. The throb in her ankle let her know she had done too much, so she moved slowly back to the sofa to prop her foot up again. Another chill rushed through her, so she tightened the blanket around her.

Gavin was still outside, and she said a silent prayer that he would find something for them to eat. Of course, he would be wet and muddy upon his return...

Priscilla sighed. He would have to take off his wet clothes so as not to catch a chill. Heavens, this was not good at all. Because of all the time they had spent alone together already, would her reputation be ruined? Would his grandmother understand? She doubted the dowager would forgive her, and by morning, Priscilla would have to return home to live out her last days with her father. Her younger sisters, Felicia and Jannette, would find husbands quickly. Both were lovely and outgoing. Priscilla had been the shy sister in the family.

Gavin's heavy boot steps on the porch brought her out of her misery, and she looked toward the door. It sounded as though he was kicking his boots against the wall. She prayed he had found something in the muddy garden.

When he entered, he was drenched from head to toe, and covered in mud from his knees down. Yet in his mud-coated hands were carrots and two potatoes.

"You found something!" she cheered.

"Not only that, but I discovered a meat room around back, and inside was some jerky." He motioned toward his coat pocket.

Not thinking about her ankle, she rose and limped to his side, reaching into his pocket and pulling out the jerky. She quickly took a bite, and then closed her eyes and sighed with satisfaction.

"Let me go back outside and wash my hands clean, along with the vegetables."

She nodded and took another bite of the jerky. It didn't take him long before he came back, handing her three clean carrots and two potatoes. As she took a bite of the potato, her hand shook as though she was half starved. She really wasn't, so why did she feel the need to forgo her manners and eat in a hurried fashion?

Gavin moved to the fire. As he ate, he shivered. Her heart wrenched. He would catch pneumonia after this was over. And it was all her fault.

She limped to him and handed him the extra blanket. "Gavin, it is now your turn to get out of those wet clothes. Hopefully, we will have enough fire to dry your clothes before the flames disappear."

"Did you find more wood?"

"In the cooking stoves."

"At least you found some." He bit into the carrot.

"But I was thinking, if it comes down to it, we could probably break up that"—she motioned to the wooden chair he had been sitting on—"and use it for firewood."

His face brightened as he looked at the chair. "You are absolutely brilliant, Cilla."

"But first"—she pointed to the blanket—"get out of your wet clothes."

She moved back to the sofa and reclined, resting her foot on the armrest again. She turned slightly toward the cushions so she wouldn't see him remove his clothes. But although she couldn't see, she heard the wet garments coming off, and could imagine what he looked like. That was not a good thing at all.

Waiting for him to undress was making her anxious. Without looking at the fire, she could tell it was getting low again. Hopefully, he had the strength to break the wooden chair apart, because she doubted she could do it.

His puffing sounded ragged, and she could tell he was shivering. "Gavin? Are you all right?"

"I'm almost done, but we will definitely need more fire in a minute. Those logs you found didn't last long."

"I know. There should be an ax somewhere around this place. I will go look for it. I'm sure you are in no condition to do that."

"True, but neither are you. And if you go outside to find it, you will end up just like me—cold as a glacier, with only a blanket for warmth."

"And," she added, "with teeth chattering loudly."

He chuckled. "Is it that obvious?"

"Indeed. I believe the chatter is echoing through the room."

He laughed harder. "I'm done now."

She turned and saw him sitting by the fire, looking shriveled with his blanket. His clothes were draped over the chair that would eventually be used for firewood. However, at the moment, it was needed to help dry his clothes.

Sighing, she scanned the room, looking for something else that might work for firewood. In the corner was a bookcase, holding only four books. "Your Grace, what if—"

"Cilla, please remember, you promised to call me Gavin."

She nodded. "Gavin, would you be terribly upset if we used those books to help the fire?"

He glanced at the bookcase. "Not at all. In fact, I might use the bookcase as well."

He trembled as he moved toward the corner of the room. The blanket didn't cover all of his legs, and from the calves down, they were bare, and very muscular. He had large feet, but then again, he was a tall man.

Feeling ashamed for admiring his legs, she tried to look away, but it was impossible. The poor man shivered so badly as he gathered the books. The blanket slipped off one shoulder, and she could see part of his wide chest.

Look away, Priscilla! And yet she ignored the warning in her head and watched him in fascination as he took the books to the fireplace and threw them in one at a time. Soon, the fire grew, but more wood was needed.

Knowing he needed her help, she moved off the couch and met him at the empty bookshelves. He met her stare. His face was pale, and his lips were turning blue. She couldn't let him freeze to death.

"Here, let me." She lifted one of the shelves and carried it to the fire. Thankfully, the whole shelf fit inside the hearth.

She turned back to him and pushed him toward the sofa. "Sit," she instructed him.

Once he was on the cushion, she sat beside him, draping her blanket around both of them. Skepticism was in his expression when his gaze met hers.

"You look like death. I'll share my body heat, but just know, I'm only doing this to save your life."

He shakily nodded and cuddled beside her. After a few minutes, she knew he wasn't getting warm enough, so she turned and wrapped her arms around him. He rested his head on her shoulder as she briskly rubbed her hands up and down his arms and back.

The fire finally put out more heat, and slowly, Gavin stopped trembling. It was strange having him up against her like this, and yet at the same time, it comforted her. Of course, she reasoned that she felt this way because she was trying to keep him from turning into an icicle. For some reason, though, she didn't want him to move. And sharing their body heat made her warm as well.

Hearing his breathing was relaxing, and lulled her to dreamland. Her eyelids grew heavy, and although she fought it, she lost. Closing her eyes, she rested her head against his. Although what they were doing was certainly improper, it felt so nice, and right now, she needed this as much as he did.

After she had given her heart to him eighteen months ago and he had fed it to the wolves, she died inside. At that time, she vowed to never trust a man again. Yet she found herself wanting to give Gavin another chance. If they were to be true friends, she must trust him.

Friends? Was that something they could do, considering their past? How could she expect to just be friends when at night she dreamed of his sultry kisses and the tender way he had held her? How could she forget his hypnotizing green eyes that had stared at her so intently until she succumbed to his adorable charm?

And pray, how *could* she be his friend when jealousy crept inside her while watching him stare at other women and flirt with them as he had once done with her? She could not control her feelings. The best way to stop this vicious cycle that pulled her into his seduction was to never see him again.

"Cilla?" he whispered.

She blinked awake, and it took a few seconds longer to gain her bearings. How long had she been asleep? The fire hadn't gone down very much, so perhaps it had only been a few minutes.

"Yes," she answered groggily.

"I want to thank you for everything you have done."

Her heart softened from his sincerity. "You are most welcome, Gavin."

"And thank you for calling me by my name."

She smiled but didn't answer.

From under the blankets, his hand shifted and slid around her waist. She sucked in a breath. What could he possibly be thinking? Had he forgotten that she was only doing this to keep him warm? Perhaps he was *too* warm, because now her body was burning.

"It takes a woman with an extremely kind heart to save a man's life." He tilted his head back enough for her to look into his eyes. "You, dear Priscilla Hartwell, are the very image of this woman. Not only did you save me from undue suffering from my allergies last night, but today, you are saving me from catching pneumonia. I wouldn't want to be trapped in this cottage during a raging storm with anyone else but you."

A lump formed in her throat, making it hard to swallow. "I appreciate the sentiment, but—"

"I promise you this here and now. I will never break your heart again."

She narrowed her gaze on him. What exactly did he mean by

that? She prayed he didn't expect her to fall for his charm again, because that wasn't going to happen. "I... I must say, that relieves me greatly."

"What I did to you the first time we met was selfish. I was so wrong to treat you so unkindly and not consider your feelings. I pray you will forgive me, because the anguish from the guilt of what I have done to you is worse than my suffering with my allergies."

Her chest tightened, and she could scarcely think of a reply. She knew his charm, but this, now... He was being truthful. She doubted this was a way to seduce her—even though if she didn't gain control of her emotions, she might fall prey to his charm once again.

His gaze dropped to her mouth, and her heart skipped a beat... or several, actually. Against her will, her breathing quickened, and her insides trembled. She couldn't—wouldn't—let him kiss her. He couldn't possibly think she would allow that, could he?

But just as she prepared herself to stop him, he lowered his head back to her shoulder and snuggled closer. He must be insane, or perhaps it was her who was losing her mind. Yet, for the life of her, she didn't want to pull away from the comforting, warm cocoon their bodies and the blanket had made.

Perhaps she was ill and didn't know it. That could be the only explanation for not wanting to pull away.

It was a good thing nobody knew about this. And she would do whatever she could to make certain nobody ever found out.

Chapter Eight

GAVIN'S STIFF BODY woke him from a pleasant dream, but when he realized he was still cuddled against Priscilla, he knew it hadn't been a dream at all. A smile stretched his lips. He didn't dare move for fear he would awaken her. But the slow and steady beat of her heart, which he had had the privilege of listening to all afternoon, told him she was still asleep.

For someone who had hated him so desperately, she'd softened quickly enough when she thought he was going to freeze to death. And to be quite honest, he had thought the same. He couldn't remember ever being that cold. However, now he couldn't remember ever being this warm before, and the fire had nothing to do with it.

He peeked toward the hearth. The fire was nearly out. He should add another shelf soon, and yet he didn't want to move. Lying against Priscilla was too nice.

A light moan rattled through her throat as she shifted on the couch. The movement brought him lying almost next to her, but now his head was closer to her chest. This wasn't good at all. As he was a former rakehell, familiar feelings of desire strummed through him, reminding him that he had once kissed her sweet lips, and they had been heavenly. He had held her in his arms, not once, but twice, and now he wanted to experience that rush of desire again.

Slowly he lifted his head to study her beautiful face. He had always thought of her as pretty, but now she was exquisite. There was something different about her now, which he couldn't quite understand. Was it because she had told him she didn't want to have anything to do with him and he wasn't used to rejection? But in the back of his mind, he knew that wasn't the reason she had become intriguing to him.

With her asleep, he could stare at her the way he wanted, the way he couldn't during his grandmother's afternoon social earlier today. Priscilla's dry hair hung around her shoulders, making her very desirable. He really shouldn't be thinking this way. Not about her. He didn't want to start something he couldn't end. And he had promised her he wouldn't break her heart again.

After he inherited the title of duke, his grandmother encouraged him to rebuild the family's reputation after his father had destroyed it. No longer could Gavin act irresponsibly, and he had taken on the task of making himself and the family name look good in Society's eyes. And if he hurt Priscilla again, he would never be able to forgive himself.

Frowning, he sighed. Which, of course, meant that he couldn't kiss her, and he especially couldn't have any feelings of desire for her. She'd told him they were friends, and so he must stick to that, even though it would be extremely difficult.

She stirred and opened her eyes. They were hazed over with sleep, but she peered directly at him. He held his breath, waiting for her to yell at him to get off her. But as the awkward seconds passed, all she could do was stare. Then... she smiled.

His heartbeat quickened. Why was she looking at him that way? And why had her gaze dropped to his mouth as her expression turned to one of passion?

He swallowed hard and gritted his teeth. She must not be awake. That was the only explanation. Yet the way she stared at his mouth made him wonder if she wanted him to kiss her. As hard as he fought the temptation, he just wasn't the type of man to turn a woman down. When desire was present, he knew he must act upon it. And in the state of mind he was in right now, how could he hold himself back?

Hesitantly, he leaned in. If she didn't want a kiss, she would stop him at any moment. Instead, she closed her eyes and met his lips halfway. Startled, he hitched a breath, while she sighed heavily. It was *not* supposed to happen like this.

She threaded her fingers through his hair, making him feel more relaxed, but at the same time, he was inwardly jumping with excitement. Her kiss was incredibly tender, and just as he remembered from their very first time, her lips were the sweetest he had ever experienced. Fire burned inside of him, and he wanted to turn things up a notch, but he should let her control the moment to see what she wanted to do next.

By the way she kissed, it was obvious how inexperienced she was. Of course, this made him want to be her teacher. Would she be an eager student? However, the only way he was going to know was test the waters.

As he shifted to get better access, he moved his hand around her waist, bringing her closer. Slowly, he took control, and thankfully, she allowed it. Being as gentle as possible and not letting his raging desire for her ruin anything, he showed her how to kiss. Soon, she began copying his actions.

Excitement built up inside him until he couldn't hold back any longer. Tilting his head, he deepened the kiss. A tight moan escaped her throat, just as her body melted. He groaned, not believing this was happening. He should stop this, but heaven help him, there was no way his mind would let him pull away.

Once again, warning bells chimed through his head, but he pushed them aside, convincing himself that she wouldn't be kissing him so urgently if she didn't want it too. She must have been as curious as he was at first, but now, without a doubt, he knew that kissing Priscilla was the most enjoyable thing he had ever done in his life. It worried him that he didn't want to stop, and even once they were back at the manor, he would still want to sneak in kisses throughout the day. He prayed she obliged him with his craving.

Another heady sigh tore from her as she ended the kiss and rolled her head away, closing her eyes. A satisfied smile stayed on her face as she drifted back to sleep.

Groaning with frustration, he shook his head. She had been asleep this whole time. Yet would she remember the exciting kiss she thought had been in her dreams? How could she not, especially after how passionate she had been?

This was so unfair! But perhaps it needed to happen like this. After all, he didn't want to break her heart ever again, but he wasn't ready for marriage, which was what his grandmother wanted. If she knew what they had done just now, she would expect him to do the right thing and propose. That could not happen, and he didn't know if it ever would.

<hr />

A COOL BREEZE touched Priscilla's face, waking her from a deep sleep. The stiffness in her body let her know the uncomfortable cushion beneath her wasn't the mattress on her bed. As she came awake and opened her eyes, she remembered the rainstorm, the cottage... and cuddling with Gavin on the sofa.

She sighed, trying not to remember it that way. They were not *cuddling*. Instead, she was trying to keep him warm so he didn't freeze to death. Yet she had felt warm and tingly inside, as though keeping him from freezing had meant something personal—as though they had done something very intimate.

Her mind flashed with an image of his face leaning in to kiss her...

Her heart fluttered and she shook away the dream. Why on earth was she dreaming of kissing him so passionately, and liking it? Although she had kissed him once eighteen months ago, her dream seemed much better. But then, it wasn't real, and it never would be. She was not going to kiss him or get involved with him ever again.

As she became alert, she noticed that Gavin was dressed and dousing the fire. She rubbed the sleep out of her eyes and sat up. She couldn't hear the rain pelting the roof anymore, and from the window it appeared that a coach was outside...

A coach?

She gasped and jumped to her feet, realizing too late that she had sprained her ankle. Grimacing, she limped toward the window. "Gavin, is someone here?"

"Yes, my dear Cilla. Grandmother sent a footman to find us."

He moved toward her and placed his hand on the lower part of her back. Warmth spread through her again, making her insides tremble. *No, it was a dream and nothing more...*

She gazed into his beautiful eyes, and her heart melted. Why was he so blasted handsome? And why did she feel differently about him?

"How is your ankle feeling?" he asked.

His voice was so deep, sending tingles throughout her body. And pray, why was her heart beating faster the longer he stared at her? Perhaps it was because her dream seemed so real. But whatever the reason, she had to stop this infatuation immediately.

"My ankle is still sore, but it is much better than earlier."

"Put your stockings and boots back on. The footman is waiting for us."

She snapped out of the trance his gaze had put her under and moved back to the sofa to do as he instructed. Thankfully, her boot went on a little easier this time. He knelt in front of the hearth, stirring the ashes.

"Gavin? I'm assuming because your grandmother's footman is here that she..." Priscilla swallowed hard. "That she knows we were together in the cottage during the storm?"

He sighed heavily and looked at her over his shoulder. "That is what I assume as well."

She licked her dry lips. "Will... my name be ruined?"

"Not if I can help it, my lovely Cilla. We were both caught in the storm, and because you were injured, we had no other choice but to seek shelter. Hopefully, when I relay the story to the dowager, she will understand."

"I... I fear she will dismiss me from my duties as her companion."

"No, Cilla. I will not let her do that."

She prayed he could convince his grandmother that nothing happened—even though something had happened inside Priscilla's heart, which she would never act upon. "I'm ready to go now."

He moved toward her again, picking up one of the blankets. "The weather brought cooler temperatures, so I insist you wrap this around your shoulders to keep warm."

As he pulled the blanket around her, she had to squeeze her eyes closed. Looking at him when he was this close made her imagine kissing him again. Frustrated with her inability to stop thinking that, she breathed slowly and deeply, trying to get her mind to come awake. And if that didn't help... she would be tempted to scream.

"What is amiss, my lovely?" His finger tipped up her chin, and she looked at him. "Is your foot causing you more pain now?"

Her foot? Yes, she must blame her frustration on her ankle. "Indeed, my ankle is still very sore. We should leave so I can get it propped up again before the swelling returns. I pray your grandmother will understand that I need to stay off it for the rest of the day."

"She will. She is very understanding when it comes to injuries." He slid his arm around her, pulling her next to his side. "Let me assist you out to the coach."

Perhaps she shouldn't let him. After all, she was becoming breathless with his arm around her. But she focused ahead of her and slowly walked toward the coach. The rain had indeed stopped, but the ground was so very muddy. The driver sat on top, holding the horse's reins, looking straight ahead. The footman held the door open and reached a hand out to help her. With his and Gavin's help, she made it inside the coach.

She sighed with relief, but then realized she still had to ride with Gavin all the way back to the manor. Alone. As long as he sat on the other bench and kept his distance, everything would be fine. But after he had climbed inside, he did the very thing she hoped he wouldn't do. She grumbled in silence. What was wrong with him?

The vehicle jerked into motion, bouncing her on the seat. She tried not to bump into Gavin, but it was impossible.

"Let me explain everything to my grandmother," he said after a few minutes of silence. "Because none of this was your fault, and I need to let her realize that."

Priscilla kept her attention ahead instead of on the caring man beside her. "I thank you, Gavin."

He covered her hand with his and squeezed gently. "And I'll tell her not to work you too hard these next few days so that your ankle heals."

She glanced at their hands, silently willing him to remove his warm touch, but apparently, he wasn't a mind reader. "I feel just awful about spraining my ankle so soon after starting my employment."

"Grandmother will understand that your horse was spooked and threw you off. I'm just grateful you weren't harmed any worse."

"I was humiliated at first." She frowned, looking at him again. "I mean, it has been many years since I was bucked off a horse. Then to realize I couldn't even stand…" She shook her head. "I'm usually not this helpless."

"As I know very well." He winked.

Once again, the pitter-patter of her heartbeat accelerated. Why couldn't he return to being the cad she had first met? But she needed to confess something, only because it would be heartless if she didn't. "I must thank you for coming to my rescue.

Forgive me for not saying so sooner."

His expression softened, which made his green eyes lighter. He smiled, causing flutters inside her belly.

"Thank you, my lovely Cilla. I know how difficult it was for you to say that."

He truly had no idea how hard it was, but thankfully, he would never know why. She forced a smile. "Yes, well... knowing how I felt about you and how mean I had been, I'm just glad you didn't decide to leave me there on the ground to teach me a lesson in humility."

He chuckled. "No. I could never do that. I'm not that kind of man."

She dropped her gaze to their hands again. Why wasn't he removing his? And pray, why wasn't she pulling hers away?

"I'm glad you wouldn't have done that. Perhaps I have misjudged you all this time." She peeked at him again. His gaze was also on their joined hands. "Gavin, you are not the man I met eighteen months ago."

His eyes met hers. "I can honestly say I'm not that man anymore."

The sweet, somber look on his face right now was genuine. She could stare at him all day. Thankfully, the coach came to a stop, jerking her out of her foolish thoughts.

He lifted her hand to his mouth and brushed a kiss across her knuckles. "I hope we have finally made amends with our past. I would really like us to be good friends. Heaven knows I need one to confide in."

His breath was warm, but his lips were oh-so soft—just like in her dream. *Stop this insanity!* "Indeed, I don't have friends here, only your grandmother."

He gave her a heart-tugging smile before turning and opening the coach's door. Relief swept over her. She was glad they could return to their normal lives. With any luck, he would leave the manor soon so that she didn't have to daydream about him any longer.

Chapter Nine

GAVIN MADE SURE Priscilla was taken to her room first before he searched for his grandmother. She waited for him in her favorite spot—the music room. Although her fingers were curled with age, he knew she still wished she could play the pianoforte the way she used to when she was younger.

As he walked inside, her eyes grew wide. "Oh, bless the Lord. You are back safe."

"Indeed, and no worse for wear." He brushed a hand along his wrinkled clothes. "I know I should have changed before coming to see you, but I didn't want you to worry any more than you have."

"Where is Miss Priscilla? Was she with you?"

Here was the moment he had to confess, but he wouldn't tell his grandmother *everything* that had happened. He promised Priscilla he wouldn't ruin her reputation, and he was a man of his word. Well, at least he was now that he had taken over the responsibilities of a duke.

"Miss Priscilla was thrown from the horse just as the storm started. Her ankle is badly sprained."

"Oh no." The dowager's hand flew to her throat. "That poor dear. Were you with her when that happened?"

"No. I had been riding, but I heard a scream, so I went in search of whoever had been hurt."

He carefully explained how he found Priscilla, and she reluctantly agreed to let him take her back to the manor, but because of the severe storm, he knew he was putting her at risk of catching pneumonia.

The more he told her about what happened, the wider his grandmother's eyes grew. It was clear by her distressed expression that she was thinking the worst. He couldn't allow that. Priscilla didn't deserve to be punished just because she was thrown from a horse.

"The stubborn woman wanted to walk back to the manor on an injured foot," he continued. "I couldn't let her risk the journey." He paused. "Please, do not judge her or find fault with her in any way. She is not the blame in any of this."

When he finished, he waited for his grandmother to say something, but the seconds ticked by without a word from her. That only meant one thing. She was trying to find logic in it all and would certainly think the worst. If that happened, he needed to put his charming skills to work and convince her otherwise.

She expelled a breath. "My dear boy, do you know what this means?"

Gavin stared at his grandmother as his throat tightened, threatening to choke the life right out of him, he was certain.

"Gavin, think about this clearly." The older woman's face was laced with sympathy as her gaze silently pleaded for him to understand. "You were with an unmarried woman, alone, for several hours. Although nothing happened between you in *that* manner, the point still remains—you were alone with her. If my servants start any rumors, her name will be ruined, and I won't be able to keep her as a companion. And Gavin, if you don't marry her, the good name you have been trying to build for your family will be all for naught. Society will say you are just like your father, only caring about yourself and your own pleasures."

Grumbling, he turned away from his grandparent and marched to the window. Instead of gazing across the wet land, he closed his eyes and pressed his head against the windowpane.

Marriage? No, it was impossible. He wasn't ready for that, and Priscilla *definitely* wasn't ready. He was just barely getting her to like him again. If he proposed marriage now, she would hate him... even if her kiss had told him differently. But she had been dreaming, so it hadn't been real to her.

"Please, Grams. Don't force Priscilla to do something she is strongly against. None of this was her fault."

"I know, Gavin." The dowager frowned. "It wasn't your fault either, but situations like this will only ruin those involved. Because you are a duke, it won't affect you much, but our dear, poor Miss Priscilla—it will indeed ruin both her and her family. She has two younger sisters that might never marry just because of what happened with the two of you today at the cottage."

This wasn't going well at all. And why couldn't he think of the words to change her mind? It was as if a fog had covered his thoughts.

He pushed his fingers through his messy hair as he turned and paced the floor. "Miss Priscilla is a complicated woman. We... had a past that you don't know about, and I hurt her terribly. She doesn't trust me." He sighed and looked at the older woman sitting in her rollerchair close to the fireplace. "What if I can pay off your servants to stop them from gossiping?"

She smirked. "You must be joking. You know as well as I do how quick they are to spread rumors. Besides, making things right with Miss Priscilla is the *gentlemanly* thing to do, and although you may not have been a gentleman before, it is time you start."

He rubbed at his forehead, which had started to pound. "I know, I know."

Gavin took deep breaths in an attempt to clear his head and think of a better solution. Sadly enough, he still couldn't think straight. He worried about how Priscilla was going to react, but he also didn't know if bringing her into his complicated life was a good idea, as Grams seemed to believe. What if he couldn't support a wife? And there would definitely be children eventually.

It was bad enough that he was being forced to sell the other estates and townhouses. Marriage was not the correct choice at the moment.

"Grams, you don't understand. My life... circumstances going on currently..." He stopped, not knowing how to explain the complications to his grandmother. He didn't want her to panic because they were running out of money.

"My dear boy," his grandmother said in a calmer voice, "you need to remember, this isn't just about you. Miss Priscilla's future is at stake as well."

"I understand, I assure you, but I just don't know..." He inhaled slower, trying to gain control over the fear rushing through him. He must be strong. There was a way out of this mess—he just had to find it.

"What if I court Priscilla first to show Society that I'm interested in her, but then, as they will suspect from my past, I don't offer marriage and move on to my next conquest?"

Grandmother arched an eyebrow at him. "Gavin Wayne Worthington! Stop this nonsense now. You are not a simpleton. Unlike your father, *you* have a backbone and a conscience. You will do the right thing."

The right thing? Wouldn't it be the right thing *not* to make the lady in question hate him? Wouldn't it be the right thing to give the lady in question the opportunity to decide what *she* wanted to do?

But Grams was right when she said there was no way to stop servants from gossiping. Gavin had been the topic of many rumors over the past few years. Some of the things he had heard had damaged his heart. *He is just like is father.* Gavin didn't ever want to be like his father. And so he must marry Priscilla, even if it would upset her.

"Fine," he whispered heavily, and met his grandmother's stare. "I'll marry Miss Priscilla. But please let me talk to her first. I want her to hear it from me. Then, if she gets upset, you can step in and convince her why this is right."

His grandmother smiled and nodded. "You have made the right decision."

"I hope so, or my life is going to be miserable for years to come."

⁂

THE NEXT DAY, Priscilla's ankle felt much better. The dowager had her physician take a look at the injury, and he concluded the same thing Priscilla had suspected—it was a sprain. Thankfully, just as Gavin had suggested, the dowager understood and allowed her to rest. However, Priscilla was tired of being in her room.

She stepped lightly on her ankle as she walked down the stairs. Her heart had lightened considerably thanks to her time spent alone, and especially because she hadn't seen Gavin since they had exited the coach yesterday. She'd had a pleasant visit with the dowager duchess, and Priscilla thanked the stars in the heavens that her employer hadn't chosen to release her from being a lady's companion. Gavin must have done as he said he would, and hopefully, there was a way to convince the servants not to gossip.

Gavin's handsome face hadn't left her mind, which was frustrating, especially after she had gone to bed last night. All night, she'd dreamed about kissing him. Now, as she thought about those passionate dreams, her heartbeat skipped excitedly. Why did it feel so real? The way her body burned, and her lips tingled, made her wonder if it *had* been real. Why could she still feel the touch of his tongue against hers, especially when he had not kissed her like that eighteen months ago? She could still feel his arms around her as they lay beside each other on the sofa, their mouths fused as the air around her became hotter than the fire in the hearth.

It wasn't real... Or was it? Could he have kissed her sometime during the time they cuddled on the sofa yesterday? They had both fallen asleep, but what if he had awakened and taken advantage of her? But for some reason, her heart told her that she had participated fully, and enjoyed every second of his teaching.

She fisted her hands and grumbled. Why couldn't she just let this go? If they *had* kissed, she would surely remember something so incredible that it melted her heart and made her breathless. It was not as though she'd had a lot of kissing experiences in her life. So why did she remember copying the way his tongue stroked hers, and recall the feeling of floating on air and never wanting it to end?

She touched her finger to her lips, and an image resurfaced in her memory. He'd had that ridiculous pink and green blanket wrapped around his shoulders. His smoldering gaze had beckoned her. She could see his neck and a bare shoulder, and wondered what it would feel like to touch it. But to keep herself from caressing his skin, she threaded her fingers through his tousled hair that felt so soft. He had leaned toward her but stopped. Yet she continued until their mouths met. He kissed her so very gently, until passion crept into her body, making her groan with excitement. That was when he deepened the kiss. Urgency swept over her, and she had wanted more. She had been satisfied in knowing that he wanted to kiss her and thrill her just as much.

Oh, heavens! Why did it feel so real?

She pushed the dream back in her mind and focused on her duty. The first thing she did was check on the dowager. As she stopped in front of her chambers and raised her hand to knock, the door opened and out walked the dowager's maid.

The woman gasped and stepped out, closing the door behind her. "Good morning, Miss Priscilla."

Priscilla found it odd that the maid wouldn't allow her entrance. "Is the dowager awake?"

"She has had a dreadful headache this morning and doesn't wish to be disturbed."

Priscilla sighed in frustration. Now what could she do to

occupy her time? Hopefully, Gavin was in his study and didn't want to be bothered as well.

"Thank you. Will you inform me when she is ready so that I can get her?"

The maid nodded before moving past Priscilla and hurrying down the stairs.

Disappointed, Priscilla wandered down to the main level. Perhaps she should read a book, but it seemed that every time she picked one up, she couldn't stop thinking about Gavin and their time in the dark library that first night.

Her heart did a silly flip-flop. The library was out of the question. It was too bad she wasn't up for riding… And anyway, would riding remind her of being with Gavin at the cottage? Probably.

She stopped at the music room. Playing always calmed her, and the dowager had told her she could play any time she wanted.

Feeling better about what to do now, she sat behind the pianoforte. She placed her fingers over the keys as a melody came to mind. It didn't take long before her fingers were brushing the keys as the tune flew from her memory.

She closed her eyes, but the handsome man's face in her mind disturbed her, so she watched her fingers instead. This particular piece by Mozart made her long for home—the home she used to know as a child, and especially the closeness she'd had with Bridget. Where had the years gone? Growing into adult women was hard and sometimes lonely. Especially now.

Before Bridget fell in love and married Lord Adrian, Priscilla and her older sister had enjoyed doing things together—from cleaning the house to picking wildflowers. Bridget shared her secrets and dreams, and Priscilla poured out her heart to her sibling. They cried together, laughed together, and even pulled pranks from time to time.

What she wouldn't do to relive those days and cherish them. There were things she would do differently, if she could, especially when it came to the two lords who had toyed with her emotions before crushing her heart. Of course, the Earl of Hanover hadn't hurt her as badly as Gavin had.

When she finished playing the piece, she felt the wetness on her cheek as a tear slid from her eye. She wiped it away, not realizing she had been crying.

"What worries you, my lovely Cilla?"

Gavin's voice startled her, but in an odd sense, it also comforted her. He stood just inside the room, leaning against the wall. Concern was apparent in his expression. She refrained from running into his arms, knowing that would just be ridiculous. But he had mentioned yesterday of needing a friend to talk with. Perhaps it would be all right to share things with him as a friend.

"Oh, forgive me for crying." She laughed uncomfortably, wiping her eyes again. "This piece from Mozart reminds me of my childhood, especially my sisters. I miss them so."

He slowly walked to her and held out his hand. She slipped her palm against his, and he helped her stand before leading her to the settee, where they both sat. He kept her hand in his, tenderly caressing her fingers.

"Tell me about your sisters."

Her heart leapt, and she swallowed down the lump of emotion clogging her throat. It was nice to finally be able to talk about her family, about the good times—and the bad—and the way they teased each other when they caused trouble. Thankfully, she and Bridget weren't as troublesome as their younger two sisters. As they grew older, Bridget seemed more like a mother than a sister. But they were close, and she missed that right now.

Gavin listened intently. He laughed when she talked about her younger sisters' shenanigans, and then he grew solemn when she told him about her father's impoverished state. Because her father had only daughters and no sons, the girls had to do the work of servants, since their father couldn't afford to hire help. She also described the humiliation of having her father tell the girls to do *anything* it took to secure them a wealthy husband.

Why, the suggestion had been so improper, it nearly killed Priscilla to even think of it.

When she finally ran out things to say, she sighed and smiled. The intense look in his incredibly green eyes made her want to stare at him forever.

He didn't say anything for the longest time, almost as if he just wanted to stare at her. However, she had to break this awkward state.

"Forgive me, for I didn't mean to talk your ears off."

He shook his head. "My ears are still attached, I assure you."

"You have been so kind to me, Gavin. Sometimes I wonder if I deserve it."

"Believe me, you do." He caressed her hand again. "I actually came looking for you before I heard your beautiful playing."

"You did?"

He nodded and chewed lightly on his bottom lip while he gazed at their hands. "I fear I have something to tell you that you may not like."

Her chest tightened. She wasn't certain she wanted to hear for fear she already knew what it was. "Tell me anyway."

He chuckled lightly, but it wasn't humorous. It sounded strained.

"I wish I knew how to tell you without it becoming upsetting."

Her mind whirled in panic. "Oh dear. Your grandmother…" She swallowed hard. "She is going to release me from being her companion, isn't she?" She groaned. "I knew I shouldn't have rested my foot. I'm stronger than that. I really should have—"

"Cilla," he said, placing his fingers on her lips to stop her chattering. "It isn't like that. Not really." He lowered his hand.

His smile was reassuring, but something was still wrong. "Please tell me. I promise to be understanding."

Several awkward seconds passed as he stared into her eyes. Whatever he was about to tell her was going to hurt her, she could tell.

He sighed heavily. "Have you ever known a woman who was caught in a scandalous situation with a man, and the man was forced to do the *gentlemanly* thing by marrying her to help protect her reputation?"

A knot formed in her stomach, growing tighter by the second. Her eyes burned with unshed tears, but she mustn't show her emotion in front of him. His past must have caught up with him, and now he was being forced to marry some woman.

Two days ago, this wouldn't have mattered to her, but now... Oh, why did she have to have that dream about kissing him? And why did they have to get trapped in a rainstorm while he had been trying to help her? But most importantly, why had she allowed her heart to soften toward him?

She took small breaths, trying to control her reactions. He couldn't know about her feelings. "Gavin, are you telling me that you are being forced to marry a woman?"

Slowly, he nodded.

The painful, heart-wrenching emotion climbing inside of her was getting too strong to tame. If she didn't leave now, she would cry in front of him. And heaven forbid she blurt out her ridiculous infatuation for him, especially when she knew nothing could come of it.

She pulled away from him and stood. "I... I wish you the best in your new marriage, Your Grace."

She spun toward the door, wanting to hurry out as fast as she could, but he grasped her arm, turning her around to face him. Tears blurred her eyes, and she cursed her weak heart.

When he noticed her tears, he sighed and cupped her face. She wasn't sure why he was smiling, though.

"Cilla, my sweet. You don't understand. You see—"

Just then, a bell from outside started ringing loudly and people were shouting in panic. Immediately, she smelled smoke. Gavin must have smelled it too, because he rushed toward the window.

High-pitched voices from the corridor echoed through the manor. *Fire!* The stable was on fire!

Chapter Ten

GAVIN COULDN'T REMEMBER ever being so panicked before as he rushed outside. Flames and smoke rose high in the sky from the back part of the stable. *What is going on?* But this was no time to ask questions. He needed to get the horses to safety.

Some of the servants must have had the same idea, because they were bringing out some of the animals. Gavin ran into the smoke-filled barn. He could hear horses still neighing. Using his arm, he covered his nose and mouth and listened for the frightened creatures. He opened stalls, and the horses ran out, heading toward the front of the stable. Toward the back of the stable, the smoke was thicker and blacker.

Every minute he was inside, it became harder to breathe. But he wouldn't leave until he knew the horses were safe. Finally, he stumbled toward the front of the stable, relieved that all the animals were out.

Immediately, he saw Priscilla. She stood in a line with the other servants as they passed the buckets filled with water from the well to the fire. Other servants ran with a bucket in each hand. The water splashed over the sides as they headed for the fire.

Coughing, Gavin tried to regain his breath as he inhaled the fresher air. But he couldn't stay idle for long. He quickly joined in the group of men who rushed from the stream with buckets full of water to dump on the burning structure.

How much time it really took to put the fire out, he wasn't certain, but it felt like hours. Exhaustion had settled in every limb of his body. He sat on the ground and stared at the charred wood at the back of the stable. How could this have happened? Stables didn't usually burn, especially since his grandmother had responsible servants. None of this made sense.

He would send for the constable. Perhaps he would be able to figure out how the fire started.

Sighing in defeat, he turned his head and peered toward the others. Priscilla stood out. Her black hair hung around her shoulders in disarray, and her gown was as dirty as everyone's clothing. A small smile tugged on his lips. Although she was probably in pain because of her sprained ankle, she was still willing to help them put out the fire. Indeed, she was one amazing woman.

Slowly, everyone headed back into the house. His grandmother would be very upset and would need to know more details. He wished he had more information to give her.

He trudged back toward the house. The first thing on his agenda would be to send a messenger to the constable. The second thing he would do was get cleaned up. And the third...

He needed to finish his conversation with Priscilla.

Another smile pulled on the corners of his weary mouth and his heart softened. She actually thought he was going to marry someone else. Why hadn't she realized he was talking about them? She had mentioned it before they returned to the manor, so why had it slipped her mind? And he was certain she didn't think their kiss was real.

Should he tell her? As much as he wanted to, he still didn't think now was a good time. But she must have *some* feelings for him. Why would she have kissed him the way she had, and when he was trying—unsuccessfully—to propose and she believed he was going to marry someone else, she actually had tears in her eyes.

He hastened his step toward his bedchambers. He couldn't get cleaned up quickly enough.

When he made it to his room, his valet already had a bath waiting. Gavin quickly wrote a missive to the constable and gave it to Stewart to find someone to deliver it.

Within minutes, Gavin was undressed and bathing. He prayed the servants had prepared Priscilla's bath, too. He didn't think he could wait much longer to finish their talk.

An hour later, dressed in clean black trousers, a white shirt and cravat, and dark gray waistcoat and jacket, he paced the floor in the corridor, waiting for her to come down the grand stairs. In his mind, he prepared himself for what he could say that would let her know that *she* was the woman he needed to marry. He prayed she would understand and accept it well.

"Gavin?"

His grandmother's voice snapped him out of his thoughts, and he stopped pacing. She sat in her rollerchair just inside the parlor. He stepped toward her, trying not to let her see his concern. He couldn't have her worrying, too.

"Tell me about the fire," she said sternly.

"I wish I knew. I have sent a summons for the constable, and I pray he will be able to find something. But the servants couldn't tell me what happened. One minute they were feeding the horses, and the next, the back wall was on fire."

Grams blew out a frustrated breath and shook her head. "Something is amiss. I can feel it in my bones."

He felt the same, but he didn't want her to suspect someone was trying to hurt him and ruin his life. "You don't believe this was accidental?"

"Not at all."

He folded his arms and nodded. "It does seem that way. All of your servants are devoted to you, and so I don't think they would do anything to harm you or your property."

She arched a gray eyebrow. "But Gavin, this is no longer my property. It is yours."

His mind jumped back to when his saddle had been purposely cut and he fell from the horse. Then there was the fact that money from his coffers was disappearing. And now the fire. Who was doing this to him, and why? And more importantly, how could he get this misfortune happening in his life to stop?

This was why he couldn't marry Priscilla. However, it must be done, and he would not cower from responsibility like his father was known for doing.

The clicking of heels on the stairs made him swing around toward the sound. When he saw Priscilla, his heartbeat quickened. She wore a lovely blue gown with white lace lining the square bodice and around her short sleeves. Still damp from her bath, her black hair appeared even darker, as it was pulled away from her face and secured with combs, leaving the bulk to wave down her back and over her shoulders. She was breathtakingly beautiful, but it was her frown that tugged on his heartstrings.

She glanced his way before quickly dropping her attention to the floor as she walked closer. It was clear that she still thought he was marrying another woman, and that knowledge had distressed her. He shouldn't feel elated that she cared for him in such a way that she was disturbed thus. The sooner he could clear up the confusion, the quicker it would be to see the light back in her pretty eyes.

"My dear, sweet Priscilla." He met her halfway. She was hesitant to look up at him, so he took her hands and caressed her knuckles with his thumbs. "Grandmother," he said over his shoulder, not looking at the dowager, "you would have been so proud of Priscilla. Although she has a sprained foot, she still stood with the others and helped put out the fire."

Priscilla's cheeks reddened. "You are too kind, Your Grace. I was only doing what anyone would have done in that situation."

"Actually, I did watch as she helped the others," his grandmother replied. "I sat by the window in my chambers as everyone assisted with putting out the fire. And yes, Gavin, I was very proud of her—and everyone for what they did."

Priscilla pulled away from him and moved to his grandmother, crouching by her rollerchair. "How are you faring, Your Grace?"

"I am upset about what happened to the stable, of course, but other than that, I am well. I pray we discover what really happened."

"As do I." Gavin stepped closer and touched his grandmother's shoulder. "Do you need to go lie down?"

"No, I'm fine."

He switched his focus to Priscilla. "If you don't mind, Grams, I need to talk to your companion. We were having a conversation when the fire broke out, and I would really like to finish it, if you don't mind."

Priscilla's gaze bounced up and met his. "Actually, I don't believe we have anything more to say."

He wasn't about to let her go this time. "No, we aren't finished. There is still more explaining I need to do, and I don't want to put it off for tomorrow."

Grams motioned toward the parlor. "Why don't you two use this room? I shall wheel myself in to the kitchen and see how dinner is coming along."

"Oh, Your Grace." Priscilla jumped up and reached for the chair. "I can take you."

"Nonsense. You and my grandson should talk. I'm sure you won't be long."

Priscilla stood stiffly as she clenched her hands against her middle. Her breathing was deep and slow. Straightening her shoulders and keeping her chin up, she walked into the parlor. Gavin followed and closed the door.

"I… I thought we had finished our discussion," she said in a shaky voice.

"When we talked about this before, I believe I confused you, and I would like to clear things up." He stood in front of her. Because her gaze remained on the floor, he lifted her chin with his fingers until she looked at him. "As I recall, you had just wished me well with my impending marriage before the fire interrupted us."

She licked her lips, and once again, her eyes watered. His heart leapt. He hadn't imagined it. She really did care about him.

"Gavin, please don't do this. I would rather not talk about your upcoming nuptials."

"Oh, Cilla, my sweet and lovely woman." He caressed her cheek. "You misunderstood what I was saying. Either that or I'm not saying it the right way. I fear I'm not used to talking to a woman this way."

Her forehead creased. "Are you saying you were *not* in a scandalous situation and being forced to marry?"

He smiled. "No, that is not what I'm saying. Although I was in a scandalous situation, the only woman I plan on marrying is *you*, Cilla. I know you just want to be friends, but..." He knelt on one knee and took hold of her hands. "Priscilla Hartwell, will you do me the honor of becoming my wife?"

As he studied her, he noticed a faraway gleam in her eyes. In a quick moment, her face paled and she lost consciousness. He jumped up and caught her before she hit the ground. He lifted her in his arms and carried her back to the settee.

"Mrs. Jones," he called out loudly to the housekeeper. "I need you in the parlor, posthaste."

It only took a minute before the servant came bustling in, her red curls bouncing with every step. When she looked at Priscilla's colorless face, the woman gasped.

"Oh dear." She hurried over to Priscilla.

"She swooned. Fetch some smelling salts."

"Of course, Your Grace."

During the housekeeper's absence, he patted Priscilla's hands and stroked her cheek. "Cilla, can you hear me? Open your eyes and look at me."

Mrs. Jones hurried back in with the smelling salts and waved them under Priscilla's nose. Within moments, she stirred and blinked her eyes open. Gavin expelled a relieved sigh and nodded at the housekeeper.

Groaning, Priscilla placed a hand on her forehead. "What happened?"

"You swooned."

She narrowed her gaze to him. "*Swooned?* I never swoon, Your Grace."

"Well, whatever you call it, you lost consciousness, and I caught you."

He looked up at the housekeeper. "That will be all for now, Mrs. Jones."

She curtsied and walked out of the room. He turned back to Priscilla and sat beside her on the settee, slipping an arm around her shoulders.

"Are you feeling better now?"

"I... don't know." She rubbed her temples. "I fear my mind is still swirling, and voices are still ringing in my ears. By chance, did you *propose* to me, or was I dreaming it?"

"Forgive me for not being more romantic about it, but yes—"

"Romantic?" Her voice lifted as she moved off the settee. She swayed, but quickly righted herself. "I don't know what you were thinking, Your Grace, but there is no need to offer marriage to me."

Gavin grumbled under his breath. He'd worried this would happen. "You don't understand, Cilla. We were alone in the cottage for several hours. Although nothing really happened between us, the fact still remains that my grandmother's staff knows we were together. In case it has slipped your mind, that is how rumors get started, and then soon both of us will be in the middle of a scandal." He frowned. "The only way to prevent that and so save our families from the embarrassment of a scandal is to marry."

Her eyes teared up again, but it was entirely different than before. This time she wore a scowl.

"But... we did *nothing*," she whispered.

The urge to tell her about the passionate kiss was on the verge of spilling from his mouth, but he couldn't do that. Not yet. "What matters is that we were alone together, and... I was undressed and wrapped in a blanket for at least one hour of that time."

He stood and reached for her, but she pulled away, shaking her head.

"Cilla, my grandmother believes it is the best for both of us, and our families, if we marry."

"Your grandmother doesn't want a companion who has a tarnished reputation, is that it?" Her voice broke.

"Don't do this to yourself. It is not like that, I assure you. She knows this is not your fault. I know how you feel, but we cannot wipe away what happened—"

She threw him a glare. "Don't presume to know how I'm feeling, because you don't, and you never will."

As she stormed out of the room, irritation grew inside him. Obviously, she was still in shock and not thinking clearly. Perhaps it was time to get his grandmother involved. But in a split second, he realized he didn't need his grandmother fixing his problems.

Irritation flowed through him. If Priscilla knew how much he was against this marriage, she would certainly hate him, so he must pretend. He did care for her, and because of those feelings, he couldn't allow her to be shunned by Society because of circumstances that were out of their control.

Gritting his teeth, he took long strides, heading after Priscilla. She was already halfway up the stairs. He didn't care if she was going to her bedchamber or not. He was going to get this issue straightened out tonight whether she liked it or not!

She must have heard him coming, because she quickened her pace. That only frustrated him more, and he moved faster. By the time she reached her room, he was upon her and was able to stop the door from being slammed in front of him.

Her face was red with anger as she glared at him. "Get out of my room."

"If one must be precise in that statement, one would say this was the duke's property," he said, trying not to let the annoyance filling him take over. "In other words, the room doesn't really belong to you."

She growled and reached for the small pillow on the loveseat. "I mean it. Get out or... or..." She threw the pillow at him.

Although he shouldn't find the situation humorous, he did. It helped lighten his anger. He chuckled, catching the pillow. She certainly didn't have a strong arm when it came to throwing.

"My sweet Cilla." He sighed heavily. "You are making a bigger scene than is necessary."

"A scene?" Her voice rose higher. "You haven't *seen* me making a scene yet. But I shall give you one, Your Grace."

She turned, searching for something else to throw at him, he was certain. But he wasn't about to let her. He strode to her and grasped her shoulders, swinging her around to face him.

"Let me make a couple of things clear." He tried not to let his temper get the best of him. "First, I'm tired of asking you to call me by my name, so please don't make me repeat myself again." He inhaled deeply. "And I am not going to put up with these tantrums of yours after we are married."

"Augh," she cried out, raising her hand to strike his face, but he caught it before it could hit its target. He held both of her wrists and placed her arms above her head. He backed her against the wall so that she couldn't move.

Her breathing was heavy, and the glassy look in her cobalt eyes was fierce, but he couldn't deny she was still a beautiful woman. Passion poured out of her whether she was angry or melting in his arms during a heady kiss.

They stared at each other for several moments. Her ragged breaths began to slow, and her body didn't feel as rigid as before. He enjoyed gazing into her eyes and watching the different emotions change in her expression. Indeed, he had never seen a more vibrant woman in his life, and at this moment, all he wanted to do was take her in his arms and kiss her passionately. But as hard as it was for him to resist, he must. Somehow, he needed to make her realize marriage was the best thing, even though he still struggled with the concept himself.

Seconds turned into minutes, until he couldn't remember what they were arguing about. She was a stubborn woman, but he could be just as persistent. Perhaps the only way to make her see that marriage was their only solution was to make her aware of what *really* took place at the woodsman's cottage. He would help her remember. He would make her see that she hadn't been dreaming. And he would do it right here. Right now.

"One last thing," he added in a calmer voice. "I want you to know that something *did* happen between us when we were in the cottage." His gaze dropped to her parted lips. "We kissed, and it was the most magical moment of my life."

Before she could argue, he pressed his lips against hers. She inhaled sharply, but he wasn't about to pull away until she remembered. He kept the kiss gentle, hoping something would spark her memory.

Slowly, he brushed his mouth across hers, urging her to participate, desperately wanting her to kiss him like she had done at the cottage. It had been magical, and he wanted more of her passion. He wanted her soft and willing in his arms.

Her body relaxed fully, but the position they were in was too intimate for him to release her arms above her head. Finally, her mouth moved against his as she answered his eager plea. When she gave up her struggles and began copying his actions, his heart soared with happiness.

He sighed heavily and released her wrists as he leisurely slid his hands over her hair, the sides of her face, and down to her neck, stroking her with exploratory gentleness. Her skin was so smooth, and he didn't want to stop as he brushed his fingers along the bodice of her gown.

Her bosom heaved in a faster rhythm, making his heartbeat race with excitement. He prayed she liked his touch as much as he enjoyed the way her body reacted toward him. With every deep breath she inhaled, his strokes became bolder.

Slowly, she moved her hands to his chest, and gradually slid her palms up his waistcoat. Now he wished he wasn't fully clothed. Then again, his grandmother would have sent him back to his quarters if he hadn't been presentable.

He wrapped her in his arms, pulling her closer as she continued trailing her palms up his chest, touching his neck, and up further until her fingers teased the hair at his nape. Warmth spread through him quickly, and he shivered with pleasure.

Gavin tilted his head and deepened the kiss. Her response was just as spectacular as it had been at the cottage. A throaty moan escaped her as she clutched his shoulders, meeting his demanding kiss. Never had he felt such excitement flowing through him than when he kissed this incredibly passionate woman.

Suddenly, a realization filled his head. If their time at the cottage hadn't started a rumor, what they were doing now in the bedroom would certainly have the servants gossiping. However, now it didn't matter. He was going to marry this woman no matter how much she protested, because he knew now that she didn't loathe his presence, and especially not his kiss.

Chapter Eleven

P RISCILLA SIGHED WITH pleasure, loving the way their quarrel had ended. Gavin had given her no time to let the truth sink in—that they had actually kissed while staying at the cottage. It was not a dream, as she had thought all this time. No wonder she couldn't get the image out of her head. Which explained, of course, why she didn't want to stop now.

Heavens, he was a good kisser, so much better than when she had kissed him eighteen months ago. Tonight, he was being so very gentle with her, and she liked that most of all. Would he be this passionate after they were married?

Marriage!

At the very thought of marrying a cad, her mind snapped her out of the dream he had put her under. Were they really going to get married? And why was she so confused right now?

"Gavin," she muttered against his mouth as she broke the kiss by turning her head, but he continued, trailing his lips down her neck. Goosebumps rose all over her in a delightful way, and she tilted back her head to give him better access.

"Yes, my lovely Cilla."

His hot whisper on her flesh made her shiver. "Gavin, we really must... stop." He had made her so breathless, she wondered if she would swoon again.

"Indeed, we must, but I cannot."

She smiled, knowing he was as mesmerized with what they

were sharing as she. She couldn't get enough of the heat rushing over her, and the way her heart softened because of his gentle manner. Well, he wasn't very gentle when he pushed her up against the wall, yet even that was quite exciting. She had been upset with him, but her attitude changed the moment their lips met.

She held in another moan of pleasure. "Truly, Gavin, we need... to talk."

When he raised his head and his incredibly green eyes looked into hers, he cupped both sides of her face. The intense look of passion in his expression made her insides quiver with delight. Her whole body felt like molten lava, and she realized he commanded her body just with his gentleness.

"We really do." He caressed her cheeks with his thumbs. "However, I rather enjoy it when we are *not* talking, because it is another way to get to know each other intimately."

"Yes, but—"

He pressed his mouth against her lips again, momentarily stopping her words and her thoughts. She couldn't control her sigh this time. Oh, this man knew exactly how to make her melt. He would be the death of her, she was certain.

She reached up to remove his hands from her face, but he linked his fingers with hers and then lifted their hands together above her head and rested them against the wall. The position made them even closer—his breast to hers, and his hips fitting quite nicely with Priscilla's. As the kiss grew more urgent, his palms slowly slid down her arms. This particular cad knew how to control her both body and mind as he kissed her deeply, thrilling her completely. She was putty in his hands, but she didn't mind at all.

Suddenly, a knock on the door snatched her right out of her dreamy desires once again. Gavin turned his head toward the door. The spell was broken, and although she knew they needed to talk, she wanted the heated moment back.

"Your Grace?" Mrs. Jones's hesitant voice came from the

other side of the door. "Your grandmother wishes your presence in the sitting room immediately."

He released a defeated sigh. "Tell her I shall be there momentarily."

His voice was husky, clearly affected by the passion they had shared. Priscilla tried not to grin, but her mouth stretched wide anyway.

"As you wish, Your Grace."

When he looked back at Priscilla, he smiled while stroking her neck. "As much as I would love nothing more than to stay right here and kiss your sweet lips—and other things—for the rest of the evening, I'm afraid my duty as grandson must come first, since I know how impatient the dowager duchess is when she wants my attention. But rest assured, after supper, I plan to continue where we left off, but maybe in a more relaxing and comfortable position."

Priscilla couldn't stop the blush from covering her face. He had a way with words, and the pitter-patter of her heartbeat hadn't slowed down since he first entered her room. "I understand."

She loved the way his gaze held hers and she could see the intense emotions inside him. Surprisingly, they matched the way she felt.

"Try not to miss me," he said with a chuckle.

"Oh, I think it's *you* who will miss *me* more." After she had said it, she wondered why she was flirting with him. Wasn't she supposed to be upset? Perhaps her body needed to cool down in order for her mind to work properly. Yes, that must be it.

He grinned. "You know, I believe you are right." He gave her another kiss, but it was very brief. "Keep those tempting lips warm for me. I shan't be gone very long."

When he left her side and exited her room, a great emptiness consumed her. Trembling took over her body and she became cold.

She stumbled to the bed and lay down, hugging her pillow to

her chest. What had Gavin done to her? The way she felt at this precise moment, she realized that she was falling in love with him. But it was different than before. Now the feelings were more intense, more intimate. She actually *wanted* to be near him. She wanted him to love her.

She prayed he would return her feelings this time. She wanted him to be the man she had dreamed about for so long—the man who would love her unconditionally and not look at another woman. But she also knew Gavin's past. A lovely woman had always turned his head.

He had better not break her heart this time. If so, she would be forever shattered and not want to trust a man ever again.

Chapter Twelve

IT HAD BEEN two hours. Two hours of apprehension building inside Priscilla's chest. She feared she would explode into nothingness if someone didn't tell her what was going on. Gavin and his grandmother had been in the sitting room with the door closed, and although Priscilla had walked—tiptoed, actually—by the room many times in the past two hours, she couldn't hear much of what was being discussed. However, the raised voices were enough to set her on edge.

When her ankle started aching, she moved to one of the chairs in the large corridor, sat down, and waited. She fidgeted in the chair and wrung her hands in her lap. Were they talking about the fire in the stable? Or were they by chance discussing the marriage Gavin thought was supposed to happen so as not to ruin her reputation? She wondered if he worried more about his family's reputation than hers. After all, her family was poor. Could the Hartwells be ruined any more than they had been because of gossipmongers?

Finally, the door opened, and Gavin strode out. Right behind him was the constable. She quickly rose.

She watched Gavin's manners as he walked the constable to the door and bade him farewell, and it surprised her to see how much he had changed. Eighteen months ago, he wouldn't have done that. Perhaps marriage to him wouldn't be miserable at all.

He had told her that he had changed, but she had been hesitant to believe. However, now she believed him. This was a man she didn't know at all, and she couldn't wait to fall in love with him.

Gavin noticed Priscilla and moved in her direction. He had been scowling, his forehead wrinkled and his mouth pulled tight, but the closer he came, the more his face relaxed, until he was smiling and taking hold of her hands.

"Have you been waiting for me all this time?" he asked in a jovial voice.

"Well, you and your grandmother, of course. After all, am I not still her companion?"

"Yes, you are. For a few weeks, anyway." He lifted her hand and kissed her knuckles. "But then you will be my wife."

Her heart leapt to her throat. "Gavin, I fear we need to talk about that. I'm having doubts—"

"What is there to discuss that we haven't already worked out between us?" he asked, stepping closer to her. "Your kiss has been on my mind since I left your room."

She really wished her heart would stop flopping around excitedly like a fish out of water. "If you remember correctly"—she lowered her voice—"we did not do much talking at all."

His smile widened, making his eyes twinkle. "No, we certainly did not, and I must say, the enjoyable moment certainly made things better."

Slowly, she nodded. "Yes, well... That doesn't change the fact that we really need to talk."

He chuckled. "I prefer the other way of communicating."

Heat climbed up her neck to her cheeks. "I realize that, but I still doubt this hasty decision."

"My lovely Cilla." He kissed her hand again. "I assure you that when I return, we shall spend as much time as we wish talking... and doing other pleasurable things."

Confusion filled her even more, and she shook her head. "*When you return?* Pray, where are you going?"

Seriousness took over his expression. "I have to go to Birmingham for a few days. I fear something has come up that..." He cleared his throat. "That I need to fix."

"Does it have something to do with today's fire?"

He nodded. "Indeed, it does."

As she opened her mouth to question him further, he quickly continued.

"Grams has promised to keep you busy while I'm gone. She is going to prepare you to be a duchess."

Priscilla gulped noisily. *Me? A duchess?* She hadn't even had her coming-out ball because her father was too poor to afford it. "Gavin, I really must protest. You don't need to marry me to save my reputation. I don't think I can ever become a duchess. I'm sure you can find another woman to—"

"Another woman?" Laughter laced his voice. "That is out of the question. And please remember that we *will* be married very soon." He leaned in and kissed her briefly on the lips. "Now, I must get ready for my trip. I hope you will see me off." He winked before moving away from her and hurrying up the stairs.

Groaning, she rubbed her temples. This was certainly a mess, and at this moment, she wasn't sure if she was excited to be getting married, or if the prospect of it frightened her nearly out of her mind. And how could she be a duchess? This was something she hadn't prepared herself for, and she didn't believe she would make the Worthington family proud by stepping into the role.

She was certainly frightened of the unknown... and of marrying a cad. She prayed he wasn't like that now and that he was finally a true gentleman. Coming into her bedchamber and kissing her so passionately, and saying the words he did, made her believe he might still be a wolf in sheep's clothing.

"Miss Priscilla, dear," the dowager called from inside the sitting room. "Would you please come in here?"

Reluctantly, Priscilla returned to her duties as the dowager's companion. During the next hour, the older woman explained what things Priscilla would be learning in order to become a good duchess. The dowager mentioned going into town in a few days to purchase more gowns, and Priscilla couldn't help but feel a little giddy. Every girl in Britain dreamed of marrying a duke, or a prince. Though even now, she didn't dare believe it might happen.

Soon, the butler announced that Gavin would be leaving. Priscilla wheeled the dowager outside to the front porch as they waited for Gavin to say his goodbyes.

He leaned down and hugged his grandmother. "I shan't be long."

The dowager duchess nodded. "I have faith in you that you will make our family proud."

Confusion filled Priscilla at the dowager's statement. What had she meant by that? Did it have something to do with finding the person responsible for the fire? If so, why did Gavin have to travel to Birmingham when the fire was started at the estate?

Sometimes Priscilla wished the dowager, and especially her grandson, would confide in her a little more. Although she was still a companion, she would be joining the family soon. Wasn't that reason enough to let her know what was going on?

Gavin moved in front of Priscilla and took her hands, squeezing them gently. "Take care of Grams for me."

She nodded. "Of course I will."

"I'm hoping to be gone only one day—however, it may turn into two."

"Godspeed, Gavin."

Keeping her gaze locked on his, he brought her hands to his mouth and brushed his lips across her fingers. Just watching his dreamy eyes fascinated her.

"Are you going to miss me?" he asked softly.

Her mouth turned dry. "Perhaps I will a little."

He grinned. "Well, I'm definitely going to miss you, my lovely Cilla."

Why did her heartbeat always bang against her ribs so quickly? His words were so sweet, but she didn't think he had wanted to marry, or he would have done so by now. Had the incident in the cottage changed his mind? He had mentioned before that his grandmother thought it was best that they marry, so perhaps he didn't want to exchange vows after all.

Oh, how she hated feeling confused. They really should have talked earlier instead of kissing.

He gave her a wink before leaving her to climb up inside the coach. She stayed on the porch with the dowager duchess, and once the coach was out of sight, Priscilla wheeled the older woman inside.

"Take us to the parlor," the dowager said. "We have no time to waste."

"Why?" Priscilla asked. "What is so urgent?"

The older woman tilted her head to the side, peering at Priscilla over her shoulder. "You cannot be serious. You really don't know?"

Priscilla shook her head. "I don't."

The dowager chuckled. "Becoming a duchess isn't a role that one just steps into. The young lady needs to be trained on the proper way to act, to dress, and, most importantly, how to speak. While my grandson is away, I will do all I can to get you trained."

Trained? Was Priscilla an animal?

She blew out a frustrated breath. These next few days were going to be agonizing, she was certain of it.

IF GAVIN WASN'T so upset about all the accidents happening around the estate, he might be thinking about his upcoming wedding, and especially anticipating the wedding night. That kiss he and Priscilla shared had him reconsidering his ideas about marriage.

He had been raised with poor examples in his life. He had been too young when his grandfather died to remember how he treated and loved Grams, but she spoke highly of her deceased husband and how much they had loved each other. Gavin's parents were definitely not in love, which was quite obvious not only to their only child but to everyone in Society. Even his cousins, whom he'd spent most of his childhood with, didn't have parents with great marriages. A few did, but most didn't.

So how was he to know that marriage might actually be a good thing? He could share his passion with one woman for the rest of his life, and if Priscilla kissed him like that every day, he would certainly find marriage as a blessing instead of a hindrance.

However, she hadn't exactly said yes to his proposal. Then again, why would she refuse? It would mean she and her family would be ruined in Society's eyes. But he knew she cared for him, and that was encouraging.

He made the driver travel through the night, and they reached Birmingham first thing in the morning. Gavin told his driver to take him straightway to the Birmingham Town Police station. The constable had suggested visiting the station to inform them about the stable fire as well as his purposely cut saddle. As the constable investigated the fire, he had found the broken remains of an oil lamp on the outside corner of the stable, and a man's boot imprint in the mud heading away from the structure and into the wooded area. The footprints were nowhere near where the staff had helped to douse the fire.

Gavin scrubbed his hand over his face. Would the Birmingham police be able to help him at all? Were two incidents enough to merit their assistance, or would they think he was talking rubbish? Then again, he did have proof of money being stolen from his account, so perhaps that would convince them.

The coach stopped in front of the police station. Not waiting for the footman, Gavin opened the vehicle's door and stepped out. The street was busy with women moving from shop to shop, and men riding through the streets, either in their carriages or on horseback. There was no time to study the people in the crowd to see if he knew anyone. He'd come for one purpose, and he would make certain he didn't leave until he had convinced the police that they needed to investigate.

As Gavin stepped toward the front double doors, he heard his name being called through the noise from the street. He swung around, searching the street for anyone familiar. Only one face stood out. Miss Georgina Burns, his half-sister.

He groaned under his breath and fisted his hands. This was not the time to exchange pleasantries, especially if he had to act like he didn't know who she really was. It surprised him that she wasn't with her mother, but a servant.

Although it would be rude not to stop, especially after he'd met her gaze, he still thought about turning away and moving into the station. But he just couldn't. Part of him wanted to see if she knew who her real father was. Sadly, that part of him won the battle in his mind.

He stood still, waiting for her to walk up to him. She curtsied, and he gave her a small bow.

"Your Grace, what a surprise it is to see you in Birmingham," she greeted him. "Are you here for business or pleasure?"

He motioned toward the building they were in front of. "Business."

"Is there something amiss at one of your estates?"

He watched her closely. Not that he suspected her of starting the fire, but at this point, he couldn't rule anyone out. "The stable was purposely set on fire at the estate where my grandmother is residing."

Miss Georgina gasped, and her hand flew to her throat. "No, you must be teasing."

"I wish I was, but I'm very serious."

"Oh, forgive me for being insensitive." Her expression grew serious. "I pray nobody was hurt."

He shook his head. "Thankfully, there were no serious injuries, and we were able to take the horses out quickly."

"Thank the Lord."

"I thank you for your concern." He paused, wondering how

to broach the subject of their father without alerting the maid who stood behind Miss Georgina a few steps with downcast eyes. "I trust you are enjoying your outing this morning?"

"Indeed, I am. Mornings are the best time, since the shops aren't as crowded."

"True, however, I'm surprised you aren't like most ladies, who don't wake at the break of dawn."

She chuckled. "Correct, Your Grace. I'm not like most ladies."

He narrowed his eyes. "And why is that, I wonder?"

"I suppose it is because I was raised differently than most ladies in the *ton*."

"Is your father not a baron?" Gavin asked, thinking of the titled man her mother had married.

Slowly, her eyebrow arched. "Yes, Lord Burns is a baron, but I was still brought up differently."

"Then I suppose you should be commended for being an early riser."

"I thank you, Your Grace. And from what I hear, you were not raised as other men of your title, either."

He couldn't stop the grin from stretching across his mouth. "Actually, I was raised just as the others—by my nanny and governess."

"Your father wasn't in your life much?"

"That is stating it mildly. I didn't even know who my father was until I was seven or eight. Mother always talked about him, but I rarely saw him at the manor, and when I did, I wasn't sure of his function in my household."

"Oh dear. That is terrible, Your Grace."

He nodded. "You can consider yourself fortunate for not growing up with a parent like that."

As she stared at him, he wished he could read her mind, but her expression was blank. She held her chin up and shoulders back. She didn't give any indication of her thoughts on the subject.

"But at least you were able to get to know him in your older years," she said.

"If you consider our short conversations *getting to know him*. But I'm certain you and your father were close."

"Actually, we were not, if you must know."

Gavin really wanted to get through this conversation so he could ask her what he really wanted to know, but with the maid so near, he didn't dare push it. He knew how servants liked to gossip.

"Then I'm sorry for you," he told her.

"It appears we have the same unfortunate childhood," she added quickly.

"I didn't care much about how I was raised, since I had many cousins who filled my days and kept me occupied. I'm sure you're aware that most of the Worthingtons in England are related in some way. In fact, I hope I don't overstep my boundaries and make you uncomfortable, but we have discovered many illegitimate offspring in our family line."

Her eyes widened, and her eyebrows arched higher. Most ladies of the *ton* would become embarrassed and let him know that this conversation was extremely improper. However, Miss Georgina's face didn't turn red, and as the seconds flew by, she didn't mention how inappropriate it was for him to speak so boldly.

Finally, she nodded. "Yes, I'm certain there are many." She tilted her head. "Your Grace, do you know if any of these illegitimate children were ever welcomed into the family?"

He shook his head. "Absolutely not. That would be scandalous, don't you agree?"

As her expression changed, he could finally read her. She wasn't pleased at all with his response. Her cheeks tightened and her lips pursed. Although she may never come right out and confess that she knew who'd sired her, the fact was... she wasn't naïve to her true parentage.

"Scandalous?" she questioned. "Pray, why would it be scandalous if the offspring wants to know their family?"

"Probably because titled lords are looked upon as men who can do no wrong, even though we both know that isn't true. Some wives of such men don't want to know about their husband's affairs. They would rather stay innocent. So keeping the secret about such children is for the best."

Miss Georgina flipped her hand. "I suppose, as a duke, that answer suits you just fine, but I assure you, most illegitimate children are just wanting to be accepted."

A feeling Gavin wasn't expecting came over him, twisting his gut. Why did he suddenly feel sorry for her? But even though she wanted to feel accepted, that didn't mean it was right to let everyone know who her father was.

"Then forgive me for being outspoken with my thoughts. And although I would love to talk about this subject with you further, I fear I need to get inside and speak to a police officer about the fire."

She blinked rapidly. "Oh, I'm sorry for keeping you. I hope we can talk again, Your Grace."

"As do I."

He bowed slightly as she curtsied, before turning and walking up the five steps to the front doors and entering.

Chapter Thirteen

GAVIN LEFT THE police station an hour later. Had the trip been worth it? Probably. The officer he'd spoken with promised to look into the matter. Gavin told the middle-aged man about the stolen money, but the officer said he couldn't do much about that—not until Gavin could pinpoint the exact way the money had been taken.

He growled and climbed inside his coach. If he knew the exact way the money was disappearing, he could track down the culprit himself.

"Which way will you be heading, Your Grace?"

Gavin tapped his boot impatiently on the floor of the coach and looked at the footman. *Which way?* He would love to head back to the estate and be with Priscilla. She always seemed to calm him when he became irritated. However, he was on edge at the moment, and wasn't ready for the long drive home.

"Take me to Rendell's first. I need a drink," Gavin instructed the footman. "Then we can return to the estate."

"Yes, Your Grace."

As the coach lurched into action, he shifted on the seat. After a drink—or two—he hoped his mind would be clearer, because as soon as he reached home, he needed to go back over the ledgers and see if he had missed something. He was sure the answer stared him right in the face—if only he knew what he was looking at. If only he had been taught to keep track of expenses. If only his secretary knew more—but the man who had been friends with the family for so long had discouraged Gavin from continuing his search. If Jacob McGuire couldn't find the discrepancy, then what chance did Gavin have?

Not long later, the coach stopped, and he hurried inside the gentlemen's club to get a drink, hoping he would see some friends. Although he wouldn't mind hobnobbing with the gents, he didn't plan on taking very long.

A servant dressed in the gaming hall's customary uniform of black trousers, matching waistcoat, and jacket with a white shirt greeted Gavin and showed him to a table. He ordered his favorite drink, French claret. As the servant left to get the drink, Gavin removed his hat and pushed his fingers through his thick hair as he glanced around the room.

From one of the tables, a man kept looking at Gavin, and within moments, he stood and walked toward him, holding a half-empty glass of sherry. At first, Gavin wasn't sure if he had met the gentleman, but the closer the man came, the more he recognized him as someone he had been introduced to... but he couldn't find a name in his recollection.

"Pardon me, Your Grace," the man said, stopping at the table and pointing to an empty chair. "Might I join you?"

Gavin nodded. "Be my guest."

The tall, broad-shouldered man with dark hair pulled out a chair and sat. "Forgive me for making an observation, but from the look on your face, I fear you don't recall meeting me."

Gavin chuckled. "Does it show that much?"

The other man laughed. "Indeed, it does." He drank the rest of his sherry and placed the glass on the table. "Your cousin, Trey Worthington, introduced us. I'm his friend, Dominic Lawrence, Marquess of Hawthorne."

Gasping in surprise, Gavin leaned his forearms on the table. "Hawthorne? I can't believe you are here. I was just thinking about you the other day."

The marquess belted out a laugh. "Indeed? I didn't know I was worth thinking about, Your Grace."

The servant brought Gavin's French claret and set it in front of him. "I remembered what my cousin had told me about his friend, the Marquess of Hawthorne, and how you gamble some of your money on speculations... and how well they turn out."

"Ah, yes." Hawthorne drummed his fingers on the table. "And are you thinking of finding something to help increase your money?"

"I am indeed. Sadly, when my father passed on and I inherited everything, I didn't realize it came with a depleted bank account."

Hawthorne tapped his finger against his empty glass. "Then the rumors I have heard about the previous duke are true."

Gavin's chest tightened with anger over what his father had done. "Unfortunately, they are."

"I'm always on the lookout for my next big venture, and I will certainly keep you in mind. If you trust me, I promise not to lead you astray."

Gavin tried not to become too hopeful, but he needed a way out of the hole he was slowly being sucked into. "If my cousin Trey believes in you, that is good enough for me." He sighed, leaning back in his chair. "Until I can find the person who is stealing my inheritance, I am in need of more money."

"Now that, I can help you with, my good man."

Hawthorne held a look of confidence when he nodded. It was difficult for Gavin not to think of the marquess as his savior, but if the man could get him out of debt, he would do anything in his power to repay Hawthorne's kindness.

Gavin took a drink of his claret. "Although I cannot do it now, I wish to meet with you again so we can discuss this in further detail."

"Of course, Your Grace. Just let me know when and where."

"Well, I will be getting married very soon, so perhaps we should meet after the wedding."

Hawthorne grinned. "Then it appears I should give you my

congratulations... or my condolences, whichever you think is appropriate."

Gavin laughed loudly, causing a few men to turn their heads and look at him from the other tables. "I have heard rumors about you, especially about your exploits with women, and I must admit, we are very similar." He paused and shook his head. "Actually, I used to be like that. I never wanted to marry, but after meeting Miss Priscilla Hartwell, I cannot get her off my mind. I believe she has taken my heart as well."

Hawthorne's eyes widened, and he chuckled. "You don't say. I, too, have heard about your activities with the fairer sex, and I'm surprised that one has captured you."

"I assure you, I was more surprised than anyone. I never thought it would happen to me."

"Well then, I wish you good fortune with your marriage." Hawthorne lifted his empty glass and frowned. "I suppose I can't make a proper toast without my sherry."

"I thank you for your sentiments, but no toast is necessary." Gavin took another drink from his glass. "I cannot stay and visit long. I'm returning to my estate, and I'm eager to see Miss Priscilla again."

"I must say, Your Grace." Hawthorne snickered. "You have it bad for this woman, so I will wish you double the good fortune and I won't keep you." He pushed away from the table and stood. "Please contact me when you wish to hear about my newest ventures."

"Indeed, I shall." Gavin finished his drink and stood. "And let me say, it was a pleasure to see you again. Perhaps my luck is changing already."

He prayed he was correct in that assumption.

※

WHEN THE DOWAGER duchess informed Priscilla they would be

going into town today, she couldn't believe the excitement that shot through her. It had been a long while since she had been shopping, since her own mother hadn't taken time to do this for the Hartwell sisters before her demise several years back, and of course Father wouldn't have wanted to do such a displeasing task. Shopping was for women, not for men.

All day yesterday, the dowager had drilled Priscilla on etiquette and manners expected from the wife of a duke. At times, Priscilla thought she would scream with frustration. She had been taught much of these lessons at a young age when her mother was alive, but the dowager acted as if she was a simpleton and didn't know anything. So when the older woman announced they were going into town this morning, Priscilla couldn't wait. She had the dowager ready faster than usual, and as they stood outside, awaiting the coach, she fidgeted anxiously.

The front door of the manor closed behind her, and she glanced over her shoulder just as Mrs. Jones walked toward them, tying the ribbons of her bonnet under her chin. The housekeeper looked at the dowager, smiling as she pushed a lock of hair away from her face and sticking it back inside the bonnet.

"Is this not exciting?" she asked. "Oh, Your Grace, I was so very happy that you invited me to go shopping with you."

"And we are happy you could come." The dowager nodded. After a few seconds passed, she huffed. "What is taking the grooms so long to bring the coach around?"

Priscilla had also noticed the servants' lateness in having the vehicle ready. "I don't know, but if you like, I could check—"

The sound of wheels crunching on gravel stopped the rest of her thoughts. Thankfully, the coach was ready.

Mrs. Jones gasped and stiffened. "Why are we going in that vehicle? Your Grace, don't you usually take the larger one?"

"I do—however, my grandson took it to Birmingham because it was all ready for him to leave quickly. I didn't know we would be going shopping so soon, but Miss Priscilla is doing so well with her lessons, I realized we didn't need to wait to buy her more dresses." The dowager narrowed her eyes on the housekeeper. "What ails you about taking this coach, Mrs. Jones?"

The servant's laugh held a touch of awkwardness. "I'm sure it seems silly, but I become panicked in closed spaces."

The dowager flipped a hand. "Not to worry, my dear. I shall let you sit by the window."

Priscilla touched the housekeeper's arm. "I understand how you feel. My older sister gets like that sometimes when she is in enclosed spaces." She looked at the dowager. "Perhaps we could stop from time to time to allow Mrs. Jones some fresh air during our journey."

The dowager nodded. "Yes, I will instruct the driver on our plans."

Once the coach stopped, the footman assisted the dowager out of her rollerchair with Priscilla's help, as the woman barked orders to the driver. Within five minutes, the ladies were settled inside the vehicle and the dowager's chair was attached to the back. Priscilla let the housekeeper sit on the bench by herself so as not to feel cramped, while she sat beside the duchess.

During their ride, Mrs. Jones chatted nervously, even though Priscilla tried to keep her voice calm to help soothe the woman's fears. The topic of discussion was the fire in the stable. The dowager shared with them what the constable had found on the far side of the stable, which was why Gavin had ridden to Birmingham.

Priscilla's heartbeat quickened from the mention of Gavin. Would he be home today or tomorrow? She prayed it would be today. It surprised her how much she missed him already.

"So nobody saw anyone on that side of the stable?" Mrs. Jones asked, her eyes wide with wonder.

The Dowager Duchess of Englewood shook her head. "None of them saw how the fire started, and of course they were all too busy keeping the structure from burning to the ground to see anyone flee into the woods."

"Does that mean…" Mrs. Jones's throat jumped as she swallowed hard. "Could it be someone here at the manor who started the fire? After all, the moment someone saw the smoke, everyone jumped into action to help save the horses."

"Oh, I pray it wasn't someone who lives here." The dowager waved her fan faster in front of her face. "I would hate to think one of my devoted servants was responsible for this."

Mrs. Jones nodded. "I will keep alert for anything suspicious with the staff. You can count on my assistance, Your Grace."

"Of course I can." The dowager duchess smiled.

Suddenly, the coach jerked to the side. Priscilla braced a hand on the wall beside her, using her other hand to keep the dowager from sliding off the seat. The housekeeper released a cry, closing her eyes as she drew a cross over her bosom. Finally, the vehicle came to a stop, but continued to tilt on its side.

Priscilla struggled to climb toward the door. "Your Grace?" she asked in a strained voice. "Are you all right?"

"I am for now."

Frightened sobs came from the housekeeper as she kept her eyes closed. Priscilla had to help, but she didn't want to leave the dowager alone. "Mrs. Jones? Can you move over and take my place? I will try to get out to see what is going on."

She figured the housekeeper's large body would help keep the dowager secure in her seat for now. But when the round woman snapped open her eyes in fright, Priscilla wondered if the servant would be any use to them at all.

"You are going to leave us here alone?" The housekeeper's voice trembled.

"I'm just going to climb out and see what has happened and lend my assistance." Priscilla struggled to reach the door. "I have been in this situation before, and I believe that a wheel has come loose. We should be fine."

Just as she and the housekeeper switched places, the coach made another jerking motion and tipped again. The two other women screamed. Priscilla braced herself the best she could. She didn't think the wheel had come off in this instance, especially because it felt as though the coach was sliding down a hill. Priscilla slipped to the floor of the vehicle, which helped her to not slide all over the place. She curled in a ball, trying to protect herself.

Squeezing her eyes shut, she said a silent prayer that the coach would stop soon. She prayed that no injury would come upon the dowager, because the woman had been through enough hardship already.

When the coach finally stopped, she opened her eyes and peered toward the dowager. Thankfully, the two women were still on the seat. Priscilla leaned over and touched the elderly woman's leg. The dowager's eyes opened, and she looked around.

"Your Grace, are you hurt?" Priscilla asked.

"I… don't think so." The woman turned her attention toward the housekeeper. "Bea? Look at me. Are you hurt?"

The housekeeper's face was as white as death, but she blinked open her eyes and glanced down at her body as she ran her palms over her arms and legs. She sobbed a sigh as tears came to her eyes. "I'm fine, thank the good Lord."

Priscilla listened closely for voices, anything to let her know if someone was coming to help them out of the broken vehicle. But she didn't hear anything. That couldn't be good at all.

"Is anyone out there?" she shouted.

After a few moments of silence, she steadied herself in the overturned coach and stood, reaching for the door. She pushed with all of her might, and thankfully, it opened. The tops of trees and the blue sky were all she could see.

"Someone help us!" she called at the top of her voice.

When she was around ten years old, she had been in a carriage accident with her mother and father. They had pushed Priscilla out of the overturned vehicle so that she could find someone to help them. She prayed she could do the same now as an adult.

She pulled her dress up to her knees and shimmied up the

wall. Reaching the opening, she used all the strength in her arms to pull herself up out of the coach. She remembered this being easier when she was ten, but she didn't stop trying. Soon, she was out and sitting on the edge of the coach.

Immediately, she saw the slope their vehicle had slid down. The ground was still muddy because of the recent rainstorm. She sighed. It would be hard enough for her to climb that hill, let alone try to help an old woman who was crippled.

In the distance, she heard the neighing of a horse. Since their horses were missing, it could be one of them that she heard. Or maybe the Lord was answering her prayers.

"Please, help us!" she yelled at the top of her voice.

"Miss Priscilla, dear. Do you hear someone?" the dowager asked.

Priscilla glanced inside the coach. "I heard a horse, but I don't know if it is one of ours or not."

Both the dowager and the housekeeper wore discouraged expressions. Priscilla glanced back up the hill. In between some trees, there was a movement. Her heartbeat quickened. *Please, Lord. We need help.*

"Hello! Is someone there?" She yelled so loudly, her voice squeaked.

The sun shone on the horse as it appeared through the trees, but this time, she saw the outline of a rider. She waved her arms frantically. "We are down here."

The hopeful gasps of the other two ladies ripped through the air, but Priscilla kept her eyes on the rider, who maneuvered the horse down the slippery slope. Finally, when the rider moved out of the sun's brightness, a happy sob clogged her throat.

"Gavin!" she cried out as tears filled her eyes.

The other two women cheered and loudly praised God.

Concern etched lines in his handsome face as he assessed the accident. He made it to the side of the coach and stopped. He reached out, and she practically jumped into his arms as he pulled her from the wreckage and onto his horse.

"Oh, Gavin." She wound her arms around his neck and buried her face against his chest, sobbing with relief.

He stroked her back and long hair. "Shh, my love." He kissed her head. "Is anyone hurt?"

She lifted her head to look at him. "Nobody is injured. We are just very frightened."

"Gavin?" the dowager shouted from the vehicle. "You might need help to get us out. You will be pulling two women out of this overturned coach, and trying to get us to safety."

"Grandmother? Don't you have confidence in me?" He grinned at Priscilla and winked. "Because I think my fiancée does."

Priscilla's heart fluttered. "Yes, I do," she whispered. "However, you can count on me to assist."

"As always." He stroked her cheek. "What more can a man ask for besides a sweet woman by his side?"

The strong urge to kiss him soundly came over her, but she pushed it away. This was definitely not the time to show her appreciation for him.

"I hope I don't lose your admiration," he said to her, then added in a loud voice so that the other women could hear, "but I did bring help."

She glanced back at the top of the hill. Now she could clearly see another coach and the man who was unbridling a horse. He didn't stand directly in the sun's light, so she could see him slightly better. She couldn't understand why he seemed familiar.

"Who is it?" she asked, but seconds later, the man mounted his horse and recognition struck. Surprise bolted through her. "Adrian?" She met Gavin's endearing gaze. "You brought my *brother-in-law?*"

"Indeed. We are cousins, and I ran into them an hour ago as I was leaving the estate to find you. Your brother-in-law said he would like to come with me to search for you and my grandmother. I hope you don't mind, but I invited them to the estate. I knew you would want to see your sisters."

"My *sisters?*" Priscilla's voice rose happily. "They are here?"

Gavin nodded. "Well, only your older sister and one named Felicia."

"Oh, Gavin." She wrapped her arms around his neck again, hugging him tightly. "You are incredible. Thank you. This means the world to me."

She loved the way his strong arms held her so gently against his body. It was too bad she couldn't stay like this longer, but they needed to get the dowager and Mrs. Jones out of the tipped vehicle.

"My dearest Cilla," he whispered. "Do I hear correctly? You now feel differently about me?"

She pulled back and looked into his glorious eyes. "Differently?"

He winked. "We shall talk later. Right now, I have some women to save."

She couldn't believe how breathless she felt, and how excited she was that he cared enough about her feelings to invite her family to the estate. Indeed, she would have to find time to be alone with him to show him how grateful she *really* was.

Chapter Fourteen

Priscilla had never changed clothes as fast as she did at this moment. Her sisters and brother-in-law waited for her downstairs, and she didn't want to keep them waiting any longer. They'd had a joyous moment of hugs after Gavin and Adrian brought Priscilla, the dowager duchess, and the housekeeper up the muddy hill and into Bridget's husband's coach. Although Priscilla was so very excited to see her sisters, she hadn't wanted to get any dirt on their clothes, but they didn't care and hugged her back.

A soft beige gauze was the overlay on Priscilla's burgundy gown, tied with a burgundy sash around her waist. She loved how this color looked on her, and of course it was one of her better gowns. The maid who had been scampering around, helping with Priscilla's toiletry, had insisted on fixing her hair as well. The maid pulled back the bulk of Priscilla's hair into a loose coil, leaving a few tendrils around her ears and the back of her neck.

Once Priscilla was satisfied, she hurried down the stairs to the sitting room. When she entered, she stopped and held her breath, focusing on the sisters whom she had missed something terrible. Two pretty oval faces with bright blue eyes looked toward Priscilla. Bridget and Felicia were the sisters who shared the same dark brown hair.

An unexpected squeal broke free from Priscilla as she ran toward them. They, too, laughed with happiness. They hugged each other again, but longer this time, since Priscilla wasn't worried about soiling their clothes.

"I cannot believe you are here," she said in a tight voice.

"It was pure fate, I tell you." Bridget grinned, making her blue eyes sparkle.

"So how did the duke meet up with Adrian?"

"The Duke of Englewood told Adrian that when he arrived home and found his grandmother had taken her companion and housekeeper into town to shop, he decided to ride out and join you. When he couldn't see the coach, he became worried. He stopped our carriage to ask if we had passed you." Bridget chuckled. "He took one look at me and Felicia and knew we were your sisters."

It made Priscilla feel special that he would take off looking for them when he was probably exhausted from his own journey to Birmingham. Of course, she didn't dare think the only reason he came looking for them was to see *her*.

"Now tell me what you were doing coming this way," she said.

"We missed you, silly." Felicia wrapped an arm around Priscilla's shoulders. "We wanted to see how you were getting along with the dowager duchess and if you were adjusting to your new role as her companion."

"While the duke was visiting with us briefly, we couldn't hold back from asking about you." Bridget squeezed Priscilla's hand.

Priscilla's thoughts came to a halt. Had Gavin told her sisters about their soon-to-be wedding? She prayed he would have given that privilege to her. "And what did he say?"

Felicia giggled and elbowed her sister's arm. "Prissy, I think you have an admirer in that one." She waggled her eyebrows. "The duke couldn't praise you enough."

Warmth crawled up Priscilla's neck to her cheeks. "Oh, I'm sure he was exaggerating."

"We shall know when we ask the dowager duchess what her opinion is."

Priscilla laughed and shook her head. "Hopefully, she will say nice things about me." She squeezed her sisters' hands. "Why didn't Jannette come with you?"

"She is in Bath visiting her friend Charlene," Felicia answered. "Charlene has been married one year now, and she invited Jannette to come and stay with her for a month."

"How nice. I'm sure that meant the world to Jannette."

Felicia snorted a laugh. "I'm sure it meant the world to Charlene, too. Have you seen her husband?" She shivered and made a disgusted face.

Laughing, Bridget bumped her arm against Felicia. "Would you be nice? Although he may not have a handsome face, he treats Charlene well, and that is what counts in a marriage."

Priscilla arched an eyebrow. "Not everyone can be as fortunate as Bridget by getting such a handsome husband *and* one who treats her like a queen."

Bridget's smile relaxed as her eyes beamed with love. "Indeed, I am most fortunate."

"And who do we have here?" the duchess asked in a commanding voice as Mrs. Jones wheeled her into the room. "Gaggling geese? Upon my word, you certainly squawk just as loudly."

Priscilla laughed as she pulled on her sisters' hands and brought them toward the dowager. "Forgive us, please, Your Grace. These are my sisters, Bridget Worthington and Felicia Hartwell."

Bridget and Felicia curtsied. "Your Grace," they said together.

"What a delight to meet Miss Priscilla's sisters," the dowager cheered. "And you all resemble each other with your perfectly blue eyes."

"Yes, Your Grace." Bridget nodded. "That was the one thing we all inherited from our mother."

"And you are married to Adrian." The dowager grinned. "I

heard about the wedding, and I'm sorry I couldn't come."

Bridget smiled. "That is understandable, Your Grace. After all, you are a busy lady."

"Mrs. Jones," the dowager said over her shoulder, "bring in some tea and biscuits. These ladies look famished."

"Thank you, Your Grace," Priscilla said. "But what about the men?"

"Don't worry about them." Bridget tapped Priscilla's arm. "My husband and the duke went to find some men in town who could bring the dowager's coach back to the estate."

"Oh, splendid." Priscilla was glad Gavin was mindful of the wreckage, but she couldn't wait to see him again. She wanted to find out how his visit with the Birmingham police went and if they were going to investigate the fire.

Priscilla and her sisters moved to the couch. It didn't take long before the housekeeper brought in the requested tea and refreshments. As they sipped tea and chatted about what Bridget and Felicia had been doing lately, Priscilla couldn't stop touching her sisters in some way. The shock of seeing them was still buzzing through her head. She also wondered how she would tell them about her upcoming nuptials. Hopefully, the dowager wouldn't say anything before Priscilla had a chance.

After two hours of visiting, the sisters walked the grounds. The rain had brought out the pink buds on the trees, and spring was in the air.

Homesickness twisted in Priscilla's stomach. She missed being at home with her sisters. Their humble home had many trees on the land. Springtime was her favorite season.

"Tell us, Prissy," Felicia said, grasping her hand. "How do you like being the companion of a duchess?"

Laughing uncomfortably, Priscilla shook her head. "It has been quite entertaining, especially since her grandson has been here."

"I heard the dowager mention that you had been on your way into town to purchase some gowns. Will you be attending a ball soon?"

Priscilla held her breath. This was the perfect opening for telling them the shocking news that she still hadn't adjusted to herself. "Not anytime soon, Felicia. I suppose there is a special occasion coming, but I don't know when it is or even if it's really going to happen." Her sisters stopped and looked at her curiously. "You see," Priscilla continued, "I'm... getting married."

"*Married!*" they both exclaimed.

Priscilla shrugged. "Yes, as unbelievable as it sounds. Apparently after I sprained my ankle and the dowager's grandson took me to the woodsman's cottage to get out of the rainstorm, we were alone for too long, and the dowager is afraid the servants will gossip."

Bridget gasped. "You are marrying the Duke of Englewood? Adrian's cousin?"

"That is how things are looking, yes."

Felicia shook her head. "Out of all the sisters, I never thought *you* would be the one to cause a scandal."

Priscilla scowled at her sister. "Felicia, nothing happened." *Except for that passionate kiss that would never leave my dreams.* "But we put ourselves in that situation, and, well... Now we have to pay for the mistake. The duke doesn't want my reputation to be ruined."

"I'm relieved he decided to do the gentlemanly thing." Bridget patted Priscilla's cheek. "However, by the way he talks about you, I don't believe he is just marrying you to save your reputation. I think he admires you."

Priscilla's heart swelled. "Well, I certainly admire him."

"Tell us about him, Prissy." Felicia grinned. "Is he charming? Did he sweep you off your feet?"

"More importantly, how does he treat you?" Bridget added sweetly. "Or will Nettie and Felicia have to come live with you so that you have friends for the rest of your life?"

Stopping her stroll, Priscilla pondered her sisters' questions. Remarkably, Gavin *did* treat her well, even when he had been upset and pushed himself into her room. She hadn't been frightened of him. Not once. And he kissed so very passionately that she had lost her mind. "No, I don't think Felicia and Nettie need to come to live with me after I am married. The duke and I became friends before we were in the cottage, and we talk well with one another."

Felicia snickered behind her hand. "Prissy, your cheeks are red. By chance, have you let him kiss you?"

More heat rushed to Priscilla's face. She quickly turned away from her sisters and started back toward the house. "I'm not saying any more," she told them over her shoulder. "So don't ask. If I feel like going into detail, I will, but not until then."

Priscilla just prayed that Gavin would come back soon. She really wanted him to get to know her sisters before the wedding.

Her stomach churned from nerves. She was actually going to do this, but still, a part of her wanted to fight it. If only she knew how to feel about this, but she didn't dare talk to her sisters—although Bridget *might* understand.

If Bridget and Felicia ever knew about the doubts going through Priscilla's head, they would find them humorous. And really, she would be laughing along with them.

THE HOUR WAS late when Gavin returned home. Once he found men to help him with the wrecked coach, he had sent Adrian back to the estate to visit with the others. It was good to see his cousin again, as well as Priscilla's sisters, and as much as he had wanted a chance to visit with them before they left for home, the coach came first... as well as trying to figure out why bad things were happening in his life lately.

The constable had dropped by the wreckage just as they were pulling the vehicle up the hill, and the man inspected the broken wheel that had caused all the mayhem this afternoon. One of the spokes had been sawn down to almost nothing. And the reins hadn't been securely attached, which was why the horses escaped unharmed. But still, the questions came back: who did it, and why would someone be doing this to him?

It turned Gavin's stomach to think someone was purposely doing this. But he knew this was all aimed at him and none other. He had taken the coach that his grandmother usually traveled in to Birmingham, only because it had been prepared and he was in a hurry to leave. The accident was meant for him.

He was very relieved that none of the women had been injured. God must have sent angels to watch over them. Only the driver and the footman, who had been knocked unconscious in the fall, had suffered any harm.

Wearily, he left the coach house, knowing that this would be another expense he could ill afford, but the vehicle needed to be fixed. That would cost less than buying a brand-new one.

His headache pounded, more from the distress of everything that had happened than his lack of sleep while traveling. Perhaps he should have taken an extra hour or two to visit Lord Hawthorne and invest in some of his ventures. Then again, if he had stayed, he wouldn't have been there to rescue his family from the overturned coach.

He rubbed the back of his neck as he walked closer to the manor. A few lamps were on in some of the rooms, but he couldn't tell who was still awake. As much as he wanted to sneak to Priscilla's room and hold her until he fell asleep, he already knew that would lead to kissing, and kissing would lead to things that shouldn't happen when he was this exhausted.

Before entering, he removed his muddy boots, leaving them by the door. Quietly, he entered the manor and went up the servants' stairs. This was the quickest way to reach his room, especially when he didn't want to run into anyone on his way. He was in an irritable mood, and he was filthy. This wasn't the way he wanted to look when greeting his guests, or Priscilla.

There wasn't any noise in the corridor, which relieved him.

He made it to his quarters without being stopped, then hurried inside and closed the door. His eyelids were already growing heavy as he walked toward his bed. Each step seemed to be harder than the last.

He opened the door to enter his bedchamber, but for some reason, the door seemed lighter. Of course, it could be that he was so tired that his mind wasn't working. But as he released his hold on the door, he realized the heavy wood was leaning toward him.

Immediately, he pushed his shoulder against it, trying to keep it upright, but between the heaviness of the door and his exhausted state, he couldn't keep it from tipping, coming down on him. Before he knew it, the large object had knocked him to the floor and landed on top of him.

The deafening sound bounced off the walls and made his head spin… or was it the pain throbbing in his skull that made him dizzy? As he struggled to push the door off, he found no strength. It was as if something heavy was pulling him down.

Gavin tried shaking away the dizziness consuming him, but it only made his head throb harder. If he could remove this barrier pressing against his head, perhaps it would help.

Trying one more time, he focused on his arms, and even his legs, lifting the door ever-so-slightly until the thick wood shifted. He took deep breaths and tried again. This time, the door moved a little more. Encouraged by the strength he seemed to have gained, he tried again, and was able to move the door off his body.

He lay on his back and breathed slowly and deeply, hoping it would help the pain shooting through his head and cease the room from spinning. He heard pounding, as if he was in the path of a stampede. He closed his eyes, and silently willed the noise to leave.

"Gavin? Open your eyes and look at me."

As though through a tunnel, he heard Priscilla's voice. He smiled—or, at least, in his mind he did—as he thought about that enthralling woman. Could she really have changed his mind about marriage? He couldn't think of any other woman he wanted to spend eternity with.

"Gavin, please look at me and let me know if you are all right."

At first, he thought he might be dreaming, but when she shook him and continued to plead with him to open his eyes, he remembered the situation he was in, and what had just happened. She must have heard when the door fell on him, and she was there to help. God bless her for caring so much.

It was more difficult than he thought, but he finally opened his eyes. Her face was in front of him, which was fine, because he would rather look at her beauty than anything else at the moment. As her face became clearer, she sighed and smiled.

"Oh, Gavin. Please tell me you are all right." She gingerly cupped each side of his head.

"I'm alive." He smiled the best he could. "But the door hit my head hard, and I have a tremendous headache."

Concern etched her features. "Mrs. Jones is finding one of the servants to fetch the doctor."

"I don't need a doctor," he grumbled, and tried to sit up, but the dizziness filled him again, so he remained on the floor. He'd wait a few more minutes and try again.

"What happened?"

"I wish I knew. I opened the door to my bedchamber, and before I knew it, it was falling on top of me." He tried to look around the room to see if anyone else had come to help. "Are you the only one here?"

"Your valet is here as well." She nodded to her right. "He is preparing your bed as we speak."

"I'm going to need a bath as well."

"Of course, but not until after the doctor has checked you over."

His chest shook with silent laughs. He loved how she cared for him. "Do you expect me to stay on the floor until the doctor arrives?"

"I do." She arched an eyebrow. "And if you knew what was good for you, you would think twice about arguing with me."

"Yes, my love. I will not argue."

Her pretty face relaxed. "Oh, Gavin. I was so frightened when I saw you lying on the floor, and you weren't answering me."

"Forgive me for worrying you so."

She glanced over at the door, frowning. "But how could your door have just *fallen* on you?"

"I'm quite sure whoever is trying to sabotage my life was the one responsible for unhooking the door from the frame."

"Then I shall have Mrs. Jones send for the constable at once."

"The hour is late. This matter can be addressed tomorrow, I assure you."

She sat back on her legs and sighed. "I have been waiting to talk to you all evening."

"Again, please forgive me for being so inattentive to your needs, my love. After we are married, I will devote all of my energy to you."

"Gavin Worthington," she snapped. "Are you making fun of my feelings?"

"On the contrary. I also wanted to talk to you this evening, but I didn't want to see you in my filthy state of dress. I also wanted to be with you without fearing I would fall asleep."

She offered a faint smile. "Now it is I who feels foolish. I should have realized how exhausted you were."

"My lovely Cilla, I hope you know I hurried back from my journey just to see you. Sadly, other things got in the way, like the carriage accident and my door."

She hiccupped a laugh. "Well, you must be feeling better, since you are finding humor in this."

"Indeed, I'm somewhat better." He tried again to sit up, and thankfully, the spinning room wasn't going as fast, and his stomach didn't feel like upheaving. "Please have Stewart help me to the bed."

Although he didn't see him, his valet stepped behind Gavin and slowly helped him up, with Priscilla's assistance. Together, they carefully helped him to the bed and laid him down.

Once the softness was beneath his body, he took Priscilla's hand. "My lovely, you should probably leave now. I'm sure Stewart would like to make me more presentable for when the doctor arrives."

Priscilla's cheeks darkened with color, and she nodded. "And I shall check on your grandmother. I'm certain she heard the crashing noise of the door falling on you as well."

"Let her know I am no worse for wear. I shall be my cheerful self come morning."

She gave him that stare to let him know she didn't believe him. "Please get your rest."

"I shall, but only because I don't want another day to go by without being with you again."

She finally smiled fully. "I'll hold you to that promise, Your Grace."

As she walked out of the room, his hopes sank. These accidents must stop before someone was killed. He would make certain to find the culprit one way or another.

Chapter Fifteen

As promised, he was up at a decent time the next morning. Although there was still a slight pounding in his head, at least nothing else was wrong. The doctor had come not long after Priscilla left the room, and thankfully, the man reported Gavin had no broken bones.

As he went through the movements of having his valet dress him in his favorite dark gray trousers and jacket, ideas of what he could do filled his mind. Of course he had been thinking about this for a few days, but he tried to compile a list of people who might want to do him harm. Sadly, the only ones he could think of were the women he had hurt over the years.

The only problem with suspecting those women was wondering how they knew where he was currently living. He doubted they had spied on him all this time. And because it couldn't be them, it had to be someone at the estate, since the accidents didn't start happening until after he arrived.

"There you are, Your Grace," Stewart said. "You are looking quite well, even after last night's incident."

"I thank you," Gavin told the valet. "I'm glad nothing worse happened. I can't be bedridden at a time like this."

"Exactly, Your Grace."

Satisfied with his appearance, he left his quarters and made his way down to the main floor to find Priscilla and her family. If her sisters were anything like her, they would not sleep until the noon hour like most women.

As he came down the staircase, he heard laughter coming from the parlor. He grinned. Just as he suspected, they were awake.

He wondered if Priscilla had told them about her upcoming wedding, and *why* the marriage needed to happen. Hopefully, they didn't blame him and believed, as his grandmother had, that what happened during the rainstorm was nobody's fault. It was obvious, however, that fate was lending a hand—much to his grandmother's relief, Gavin was certain.

When he stepped inside the room, the women turned their heads toward him. But it was Priscilla's face that he was happy to see. She wore a baby-blue day dress with a square neck bodice, and her hair was fixed in ringlets. Today, she did not resemble a lady's companion. Instead, she looked most desirable and tempting.

"Your Grace," Priscilla said, quickly rising from her seat on the sofa. "I'm most happy to see you up so early. You look recovered from your accident last night."

"I am recovered, thank you." He glanced at the two other ladies. "And good morning to you. I'm glad that you have not left yet."

Bridget nodded. "Thank you, Your Grace. We plan on leaving this afternoon."

"I pray you can postpone it a few hours. I was in hopes that you would like to accompany us into town to purchase your sister some gowns."

Priscilla's eyes widened. "We are?"

"Of course. Your trip was ruined because of the wheel coming off the coach, so I thought we could try our outing again. This time, I will ride my horse at the side of the vehicle and make sure nothing like that happens again."

Priscilla stepped closer to him and gingerly touched his arm. "If you aren't feeling like traveling, we can postpone the trip."

It pleased him immensely to see the concern on her face, especially when the first two days he was here, she'd looked at him with steely blue eyes full of hatred. It softened his heart to know that she didn't loathe him any longer.

"Absolutely not, Miss Priscilla. I assure you, I feel just fine."

"Do you need to eat the morning meal first?" she asked.

"I had a bite in my room while getting ready for the day." He looked at Bridget. "My lady? Is your husband around? Perhaps he would enjoy an outing."

Bridget nodded. "He is taking a walk around the estate."

"Splendid—while you ladies prepare to ride into town, I shall find Lord Adrian."

They all curtsied as he left the room. He didn't know if Adrian would enjoy going into town, but the way those two looked at each other with admiration in their gazes, Gavin knew Adrian would follow Bridget to the ends of the earth. Would he eventually feel the same way about Priscilla? After all, Adrian hadn't wanted to marry either, and look at the man now.

It didn't take long to find Adrian out by the stable, inspecting the damage. As Gavin approached his cousin, he could tell the man was deep in thought as he stared at the charred wall, rubbing his chin. Adrian must have noticed him approach, because he snapped his head toward Gavin.

His eyebrows arched. "What are you doing out of bed? From what I heard, I would expect you to be recovering."

Gavin flipped a hand through the air. "When have you ever known me to sit still for very long? Besides, I feel well enough to be out and about. In fact, I am taking my soon-to-be bride into town to purchase her some clothes. You and your wife and Miss Felicia are invited as well."

"Indeed, we would love to join you." Adrian nodded toward the wall. "May I ask what you are planning to do with the stable?"

"Rebuild it, of course. But my inheritance is diminishing a little every day, so I'm sure it will take some time."

Adrian folded his arms and rocked back on the heels of his

boots. "Would you be offended if I offered to pay for the repairs?"

Gavin scowled. "Cousin, it offends me that you don't think I can find the funds to do it myself."

"Did I say such words? I did not, and I never would. All I'm doing is offering to help. I assure you, I can afford it." Adrian shrugged. "Consider it a wedding gift, if you will, but I would very much like to help."

"I thank you for the offer, but I would feel less than a man if I accepted."

Adrian nodded. "I understand. So in that case, let me introduce you to a good friend of mine. He is the Marquess of Hawthorne."

Gavin laughed heartily. "Hawthorne is your friend as well as Trey's?"

Adrian chuckled. "I'm certain Hawthorne is friends with many lords."

"Well, I have already talked to him, and we will meet again after my wedding. He promises to find me the right venture to invest in."

Adrian patted Gavin's shoulder. "If anyone can help you, it's Hawthorne."

As Gavin walked back toward the manor with his cousin, he felt better about the decision to invest. Perhaps his luck was changing after all.

PRISCILLA DIDN'T KNOW what she would do once her sisters left. It was so nice having them here. It seemed too long since they could giggle like schoolgirls. But it meant the world to her that Gavin had included them in her shopping spree. Bridget knew just what things Priscilla would need for her wedding, and for those events where she would be presented as the Duchess of Englewood.

As she stood in one of the dress shops while the seamstress measured her, she couldn't help but think about everything that Gavin had done for her since she became his grandmother's companion. Although her family was way beneath his, he had never treated her as anything less than a lady. He showed her many times that he cared about her opinion, especially if she would forgive him for his past misdeeds.

She thought about the way her heartbeat quickened, making her smile more, and she wondered if she had finally fallen in love with him. Did he return her feelings? Would he make her a perfect husband? Seeing Bridget and Adrian together made Priscilla want a marriage like theirs, and she prayed this would finally be her turn for happiness.

"Prissy," Felicia said, nudging her arm and pointing toward the shop's window. "Who is that woman talking with the duke?"

Priscilla swung her head toward the window. Although she glimpsed Gavin's back and wide shoulders, she couldn't see much of the person in front of him. All she could see was that the woman wore a yellow bonnet that matched her day dress.

"I can't see her well enough," she told her sister. "Why do you ask?"

"Because I have heard how charming the duke is, especially to women, and I wanted to make certain he wasn't flirting with someone else right before your wedding."

Doubt snuck inside Priscilla's heart and made her stomach twist. She knew Gavin better than her sister, and he *had* been that kind of man. But was he now?

She glanced at the seamstress, who was placing pins in the hem of her gown. "Will you excuse me for a moment?"

The woman nodded and withdrew. Priscilla stepped down from the small platform and slowly moved toward the window, hoping to see the other woman more clearly. The closer she came, the more her stomach rolled.

When she could see the woman's face, recognition hit. Miss Georgina had been with her mother at that soiree the dowager had not long after Priscilla became her companion. And she recalled the way Miss Georgina boldly stared at Gavin.

Jealousy filled Priscilla, and she quickly turned to head back to the platform. She wanted to believe Gavin would be faithful to her after they were married, so why couldn't she fully trust him? He hadn't shown her any reason why he would stray.

"Do I need to have a talk with that lady?" Bridget asked in a soft voice.

Priscilla forced a laugh and shook her head. "Why would it matter? He is the duke, and he talks to many people. Are you going to forbid him to talk to pretty young ladies after we are wed?"

Bridget gave her that big-sister stare, and Priscilla could read her thoughts. She was only trying to protect Priscilla's heart.

"I'm fine," she told her sisters. "The duke is a very friendly man, and he will not do anything to hurt me." At least, she hoped.

For the rest of the afternoon, she couldn't get the vision of Miss Georgina out of her mind. The lady was lovely, with wavy, dark brown hair and flashing green eyes. Although there wasn't an outward flirtation that Priscilla could see, she knew how attractive Gavin was and how his charming smile could melt any woman. She also remembered how much he was attracted to women who fell all over themselves to get his attention.

Priscilla walked with her sisters to the milliner's shop, and Bridget's excitement hastened her steps. Priscilla had never liked bonnets, but she realized it would be expected of her to wear them as the next Duchess of Englewood. She didn't hurry into the shop, instead taking her time.

A familiar face caught her attention, and she groaned. Why did she have to spot Miss Georgina *again*? Once a week was plenty, but twice on the same day?

Thankfully, the woman wasn't chatting with Gavin again, but she was talking with a man who appeared to be in his forties. A few white hairs streaked through his brown hair. The woman didn't notice Priscilla, and although she should walk past Miss Georgina and enter the milliner's shop, curiosity got the best of her, making her take slower steps.

What caught her interest was the irritated expression on Miss Georgina's face. Priscilla couldn't quite see the man's face, but at this point, she didn't dare turn her head to look. She was certain he would notice that she was trying to eavesdrop.

"You need to do something," Miss Georgina grumbled. "How am I supposed to find a husband if I cannot wear a new gown to Lady Moore's ball next week?"

Priscilla rolled her eyes, grateful that she hadn't been raised to think new gowns were the sole method of finding a husband.

"And I told you before, there is no way that I can get the money. Not when he's keeping track of everything now. He questions me about every little expenditure. He will notice if a large sum is missing."

The woman *humphed* and stomped her foot. "Why? He never noticed before."

"I'm sorry, Miss Georgina, but I dare not risk it this time. You will have to wear one of the gowns you purchased last month."

"You will be the reason I cannot find a husband," she snapped.

Sadly, Priscilla had to enter the shop now. Then again, she didn't want to watch any more of Miss Georgina's tirade just because she couldn't buy a new dress.

As Priscilla opened the door and walked inside the shop, she glanced over her shoulder to get a better look at the man, who she guessed was Lord Burns, but since she'd never met him, she couldn't be certain. He *was* somewhat familiar, but Priscilla couldn't put her finger on where she had seen him before.

She thought about asking Bridget, but then realized she really didn't care about Miss Georgina or the man. As long as that woman kept her husband-hunting claws off Gavin, Priscilla would be happy.

She and her sisters didn't spend very long in the milliner's before they moved on to another one. Soon, Gavin and Adrian came to collect the women and take them back to the estate.

Priscilla fought back tears when she had to say goodbye to her sisters. Thankfully, they would come to her wedding, so at least she would see them again soon. With any luck, by then, she would know Gavin's true feelings for her and the wedding. At least, she hoped.

Once her sisters left with Adrian, Gavin made his excuses so he could tend to the burned stable in preparation for the rebuilding. Although she wanted to talk to him, she needed to check on the dowager. After all, Priscilla was still her companion. At least for a few more days.

The dowager had more lessons to teach Priscilla, but she couldn't concentrate, and several times she had to ask the woman to repeat what she'd said. The dowager laughed and accused her of having dreamy thoughts about the upcoming wedding.

If only she could confide in the dowager, but Priscilla wasn't sure the woman wanted to hear how she still harbored some doubts about Gavin's sincerity, or how she didn't know if she could fully trust him not to break her heart again.

Evening came, and after she helped the dowager into her bedchamber to retire for the night, Priscilla wandered through the manor, searching for Gavin. He hadn't been at the supper table, and she knew if she couldn't talk to him now, she wouldn't be able to sleep tonight. No matter how late it was, she had to talk to him one way or another.

When she couldn't find him, she walked to her bedchamber and ordered a bath to be drawn. Bathing had always been the time when Priscilla could think rationally. There wasn't anything to interrupt her thoughts, and soaking in the warm water was soothing for her nerves and mind.

The maid helped Priscilla wash her hair and then left. While she ran the sponge over her arms and legs, her thoughts drifted again to Gavin. What would their wedding night be like? The few times they had passionately kissed, he had made her breathless.

She wanted more, but as innocent as she was, she wasn't sure what *more* she could have. Gavin would teach her, she was certain of it.

She shook the thoughts out of her head and climbed out of the tub. Why was she punishing herself this way? Until she knew for certain what he expected from their marriage, then—and only then—would she know if giving her heart to him was the best course of action.

She prayed it was.

Chapter Sixteen

AFTER GAVIN'S BATH, he dressed in trousers and shirt, but that was all. He wasn't ready to retire for the night, and yet he had nothing else to do. He debated whether he should seek out Priscilla's company, but since it was so late in the evening, he figured she had already gone to bed for the night. Now, with their guests gone, perhaps he would find more alone time with his soon-to-be bride.

The fire was nearly out, so he knelt in front of the hearth and took the poker, stirring the embers to extinguish it. Adding another log was pointless, since the room was warm enough, and of course he wasn't planning on staying up all night.

When a small knock came on his door, he paused and glanced in that direction. Why would someone be coming to his room at this hour? He set the poker up against the wall, moved to the door, and stopped. "Who is it?"

"Your Grace, it is Mrs. Jones. I was wondering if you would like me to bring you some food, since you missed supper."

He opened the door. The plump woman smiled at him and curtsied.

"Forgive me for interrupting you," she continued, "but I'm ready to retire for the night, and I wanted to make sure you were taken care of."

"I thank you, Mrs. Jones, but I'm not hungry. Please, go to

bed. You have had a rather busy day keeping our guests happy. I shall be fine."

"You have also been busy today, which is why I offered to bring a tray of food up to you."

He nodded. "And I will retire soon, so food is not needed. Goodnight."

"Goodnight, Your Grace."

The woman curtsied and moved down the corridor. He watched her leave before withdrawing into his room, but out of the corner of his eye, he saw something white dart around the corner at the other end of the hall. Curious about who might be sneaking around after dark, he took soft steps. Just as he reached the end of the hall, a fluff of a white night rail and black hair suddenly whipped around the corner and ran right into him.

Priscilla gasped and stumbled. He gripped her arms to keep her from falling over. When she raised her gaze and met his, her face grew a brilliant red. He grinned.

"Why, if it isn't my lovely Cilla. What has you wandering around the house so late?"

A grin stretched across her face. "I couldn't sleep. The visit with my sisters and going shopping made feel like I was young again."

He caressed her warm cheek, loving the way her face lit up with excitement. "And I'm glad you were able to get that opportunity." He glanced down the corridor, making sure the housekeeper hadn't returned before he looked back at Priscilla. "However, I don't believe this is the way to your bedchambers. Or have you forgotten?"

Her face turned brighter. "No, I haven't forgotten. I was actually..." She licked her lips. "I was coming to see if you were awake. I need to talk to you."

His heartbeat quickened. "Then by all means." He motioned toward his door. "Please come in so we can... *talk*."

The blooming color of her face brightened even more as she walked with him into his room. Since there was no reason that the servants should know about his late-night visitor, he closed the door. She stood clasping and unclasping her hands against her middle as her gaze jumped around his room.

He stepped closer, and she met his gaze. She was so very lovely with her hair hanging around her shoulders and down her back, and the look in her eyes hinted of her desire for him.

If only he wasn't trying to prove to her that he was a gentleman and not a rogue… He tried to steady his breathing and squash the thoughts filling his head right now.

"I missed you today," he said, stroking her hair. "I'm sorry we didn't spend much time together."

She smiled. "I would say I missed you, but my sisters took up all of my time."

He chuckled. "As it should be."

"But I do wish we could have spent more time together."

"As do I, but I had things to do in getting the coach repaired and the stable's wall rebuilt."

"Were you able to accomplish these tasks?"

Sighing, he stopped her wringing hands by taking them in his. "My darling Cilla, you didn't come to my room this late at night just to ask about my projects, did you?"

Her shoulders relaxed slightly. "No."

"Then I beg you, please say what is on your mind." He hoped it led to kissing. If not, he would certainly turn the conversation in that direction.

She nodded. "I must tell you how wrong I was about you."

That wasn't something he'd expected her to say, and he couldn't wait for her to continue. "I'm grateful for that… I think."

She laughed. "Forgive me if I have lost my words, but what I have to say is positive, I assure you."

"Splendid." He caressed her hands. "Then tell me."

"Since you hurt me eighteen months ago, I put up a wall around my heart. When I realized you were the dowager's grandson, I wanted to hate you that much more for trying to ruin my life. However, some of your actions made me pause in my judgment. Although you may still have roguish tendencies, I believe you have indeed changed for the better."

His heart softened. He brought her hands up to his mouth and kissed her knuckles. "I'm so very happy to hear you say that, because I believe I have changed."

"You were so very selfish when I first met you, but I can see that you do care for others. You showed me that by the way you treated me, and treated my sisters while they were here."

She was correct to think that he had been selfish before his father died. Inheriting the title made him grow up so much, and so quickly. But he did enjoy the attention he received when he did kind deeds versus selfish acts.

"It is difficult to admit," he said, "that I was so heartless before, and I hurt so many people. I thank you for giving me another chance to get to know you. I was blind when we first met, and I didn't give myself time to get to know the sweet woman with a loving heart."

She tilted her head. "Indeed? You think I have a loving heart?"

"Of course, my love. Look at the way you have helped my grandmother. And let us not forget when you tried to help the staff put out the fire, all the time with a sore ankle. And then when you tried to rescue my grandmother and her housekeeper single-handedly. They both sang your praises after the accident. And I'll be forever in your debt with how you assisted me when my allergies were bad, and when I was knocked down by a fallen door."

Her smile grew. "I'm so very relieved that you believe such things about me, but I fear you may change your mind when I confess something else to you."

There was more? He hoped it was something he wouldn't get upset over. Then again, with this woman, it was easy to forgive. "What is it?"

She inhaled slowly, then released it. "The other day, with the kitten and your allergies?"

"Yes."

"A while ago, I had heard a rumor that you were allergic to cats, but I didn't believe it." She shrugged. "At that point in my life, I had heard many rumors about you that were probably not true. Anyway, I purposely put the animal in your arms to see if you had a reaction."

In any other situation, her confession would have upset him, but he understood why she had done it. And it made him appreciate her more for telling him the truth. She trusted him enough to tell him, and now he must be honest with her.

"And you clearly saw what happens when I'm around cats," he said.

"Yes, and I feel just awful that I did that to you. I hope you will forgive me."

He slowly wrapped his arms around Priscilla, pulling her against him. "After what I did to you eighteen months ago and you forgave me, I think this indiscretion of yours is very minimal."

"Thank you, Gavin. You are wonderful."

"No, you are. You have been able to accomplish something that all the other women I have been with have failed at."

Her palms rested on his chest. "What is that?" she whispered.

"You have opened up my heart and crawled inside." He bent his head and brushed his lips across her cheek. "Cilla, you have made me fall in love for the first time in my life."

She blinked rapidly, and her eyes filled with tears. "You love me?"

He nodded. "More than I thought I could love anyone."

"So you…" She cleared her throat. "You are not interested in other women?"

Her question caught him off guard, and he laughed. "How could any woman turn my head when you are the one I constantly think about and who will be forever in my heart? I promise you, here and now, that no other woman will be as amazing as you."

Sighing, she relaxed in his arms and turned her head as her

lips met his. He kissed her with all the love that continued growing in his heart.

For many years, he had trampled on women's hearts, never knowing the glorious feeling of loving anyone. The way his speeding heartbeat took control of his emotions made him breathless, yet it was the best feeling in the world.

❧

PRISCILLA COULDN'T BELIEVE what she'd heard, and yet her heart had heard it so clearly that it swelled with happiness. She had felt herself falling in love with him since they were in the dark library that first night, but mistakes and heartaches from her past had kept her from experiencing love to the fullest.

Gasping, she wrapped her arms around his neck and met his mouth with eager kisses. She clung to him, not getting enough... not ever wanting to get enough of this incredible man. No longer was she hesitant about marrying him—instead, she anticipated the moment they would become husband and wife. And by the way she responded to his kisses and his touch, she wondered if they would begin their wedding night right now. After all, they would be married very soon.

"Gavin," she sighed, tilting her head back, which only made him trail kisses down her neck. Warm shivers cascaded over her, and she smiled.

As he continued to kiss her, she wondered if she should make the hint about taking her to his bed, since it would be much more comfortable there. But somewhere in the room, she heard footsteps, and then the floor creaked. Gavin must have heard it too, because his body tensed.

The floor squeaked again, and he broke the contact between them, whipping around, toward their intruder. As Priscilla's vision adjusted to the shadows in the room, she noticed a movement coming toward them. The shadow grew, and Priscilla saw a woman's blue gown, and then the pistol she held in her hand.

Gavin moved in front of her, and she clutched the back of his shirt. His body felt as stiff as hers.

"Mrs. Jones?" he asked in a tight voice. "What are you doing in my room... and pointing a pistol at me?"

"Do you honestly believe I'm going to allow you any kind of happiness now?" The woman's face scrunched in anger. "Men like you do not deserve to be happy."

He shook his head. "Mrs. Jones. I fear I don't know what I have done to you to make you this way."

"*Mrs. Jones?*"

The housekeeper released a cackle that made Priscilla's skin crawl with terror. But then the woman pulled the pins out of her tight bun, and her brown hair fell in waves around her shoulders.

"Look again, *Your Grace*. I was much thinner three years ago when you took advantage of me. Back then, my name was Miss Jane Eggert, and you convinced me that we were going to Gretna Green to marry." Tears filled the woman's eyes. "I believed you, and so I let you have your way with me." The housekeeper took a deep breath and blinked away the tears. "Because you ruined my life, I gained weight. I had to move far away and change my name. I let everyone think I was the widow Mrs. Beatrice Jones."

Priscilla groaned silently and pressed her forehead against Gavin's arm. How many times had she thought about revenge? Gavin had broken her heart, too. And now... would he be able to walk away from this grave mistake?

Chapter Seventeen

GAVIN FISTED HIS hands by his sides and gulped down a hard swallow. Why hadn't he seen Miss Jane Eggert in the woman who had become his grandmother's housekeeper? But back then, the woman wasn't worth remembering. Now he wondered how many other women he had forgotten about. Thankfully, Priscilla had stayed on his mind. Would his dark past always come to haunt him and ruin his future happiness?

"Gavin Worthington, you are a very horrible man, and since you came back to this estate, I have been doing all that I can to hurt you and make you pay for breaking my heart."

He scowled. "It was *you* who was doing all those things?"

"Indeed, I am responsible, but fortune was not on my side. When you fell off your horse because of the cut saddle girth, you were not injured. You were supposed to die in the fire while trying to put it out. And *you* were supposed to take the coach with the broken wheel. Not to mention the door should have been heavy enough to crush your skull."

Inwardly, he groaned. Many people had suffered because she wanted revenge. Why couldn't she see she was just as guilty as he was?

"You must believe me," he told the older woman, "that I'm a different person now. I'm so sorry for how I hurt you, and I probably deserve every bad thing that you have done to bring me harm. However, I wasn't the only one injured, and that is on you." He paused, remembering one more thing. "Are you also the one stealing money from my coffers? If so, I want to know how you can accomplish this without my knowledge."

She arched an eyebrow. "I will not take credit for stealing from you. I assume one of the other women you have hurt is taking your money."

"I don't believe you," he growled.

"Your Grace, you are obviously not thinking clearly. If I was stealing your money, would I be working for your grandmother?"

Anger filled him. "I certainly deserve your wrath, Miss Eggert, but Miss Priscilla does *not* deserve any of this, and the servants of my grandmother's estate didn't deserve the labor they all went through trying to put out the fire. My poor, defenseless grandmother could have died in the coach accident, just as you."

She lifted the pistol and steadied her aim. "You are correct, and I realized my folly, which is why I decided to shoot you instead. At least I know that nobody else can be hurt."

"Mrs. Jones, wait." Priscilla tried to move past him, but Gavin held her behind him, trying to keep her from accidentally taking the bullet meant for him. Instead, she peeked around him. "Mrs. Jones, you are not the only woman he hurt with his roguish lies. I, too, was one of his many heartbroken women, but I have seen what a good man he is now. All those things he did in the past should stay buried. We have all changed since then, especially Gavin. Why can you not forgive him as I have?"

Jane smirked as a nerve in her cheek jumped. "It is clear that you were not hurt as badly, since you fell for his false charms so easily this time."

"You have it wrong, Mrs. Jones. Gavin has proven his worth to me this time. He has really changed."

The other woman glared. "He is an excellent chameleon, then."

Gavin sighed as sadness came over him. There would still be some people in his life that would never believe he was sorry for his misdeeds. He certainly couldn't prove to all of them how he had changed. But hopefully, there were enough people in his life that loved and trusted him enough to stay by his side.

"Jane, I have already asked your forgiveness, but I cannot force you to give it to me. If you choose to believe the worst, then so be it. But killing innocent people is not the answer. That will only get you thrown in the gaol. Is that something you really want? You have been a good friend to my grandmother and the other staff at the estate—do you want to lose that just because you want revenge against me?"

Different emotions played on her expression, and Gavin prayed she would seriously think about his words and make the right decision, one that didn't get him or Priscilla killed. But when the woman's face turned hard again, his hopes dropped.

"Then I suppose," Jane said in a harsh voice, "that I will be punished for my sins. But believe me, ending your life will make everything worth it."

"No!" Sobbing, Priscilla struggled as she tried to reach for Mrs. Jones, but Gavin wouldn't let the woman he loved take a bullet for him.

The gunshot echoed in the room. Gavin closed his eyes, waiting for the pain from the bullet to weaken him. But when he felt nothing, he opened his eyes. Blood covered Mrs. Jones' shoulder, spreading quickly down her arm. Her face was pale, and her eyes were wide from shock. The pistol dropped to the floor, unfired.

At his bedchamber door, his grandmother stood with a smoking pistol still in her hands. The betrayal and anger on her face as she glared at Jane said it all. Gavin's heart wrenched with emotion for what his grandmother must be feeling.

Priscilla gasped and ran to his grandmother. Just as Cilla reached the old woman, the dowager sagged against her.

"Oh, Your Grace," Priscilla said in a sorrowful voice. "How did you know your housekeeper would be here?"

Gavin grabbed the weapon off the floor as Jane sank to her

knees, clutching her bleeding shoulder. He stepped to his grandmother and kissed her forehead. "Are you all right?"

"Yes, dear," she said, patting his cheek. "I wasn't sure if these accidents came from Mrs. Jones, but tonight she said things that made me wonder, so I followed her the best I could without my rollerchair."

"Let me help you sit while I fetch your rollerchair," Priscilla said as she assisted the dowager to the closest seat.

"Gavin?" his grandmother asked weakly. "Please fetch Martin, posthaste. He will be able to find some servants to clean up the bloodied floor and to keep Mrs. Jones from dying. He will also be able to fetch the constable."

"Yes, Grams."

Before Gavin left, he met Priscilla's watery gaze. She smiled at him with quivering lips and mouthed, *I love you.*

His heart soared with happiness. This evening's events had ended rather poorly, but knowing she returned his love made everything better.

※

PRISCILLA'S EYELIDS WERE heavy. The long day, and even longer night, had worn on her already frazzled nerves, and she couldn't stay awake a moment longer. But she waited for the constable's arrival to tell him what had happened, along with Gavin and the dowager. Thankfully, Mrs. Jones—Jane Eggert—would surely go to prison for attempted murder.

She shrugged out of her night rail and dragged herself on tired feet toward her bed. As soon as she hit the mattress, she sank down and closed her eyes. She didn't care that she wasn't lying the correct way, or that blankets were not covering her—she was too exhausted to do anything about it.

Listening to the popping embers from the fire lulling her to sleep, she thought about what had happened in Gavin's bedchambers, and especially those things he had said. Although she suspected he wondered about the so-called accidents happening around the estate, he had never really acted too worried about them. He'd brushed them off as if it were normal to have a coach wheel come loose, a fire in the stable, and, especially, a door fall on him.

Why hadn't she realized he was trying to protect her from these incidents? Why couldn't she tell how worried he had been? Perhaps *he* wasn't selfish any longer, but now she felt like a self-centered person for not noticing his distress.

For sure, first thing in the morning, she would put her worries aside and concentrate on repaying his kindness. She would love him as his future duchess, and put him first in her life, as it should be. She would make him see that she loved him wholeheartedly.

Although her limbs were weary, her overactive mind still couldn't fall asleep. She didn't know if he was still giving his statement to the constable or not, but she knew she had to tell Gavin that he could trust her with anything, and she would help him... because she loved him.

As difficult as it was, she pushed herself off the bed, shrugged on her night rail, and stepped to the door. Just as she placed her hand on the doorknob, someone knocked. She jumped and gasped. But there could only be one person who would come to her room this late at night.

She yanked the door open. Gavin's fist was still lifted to knock. His eyes widened, and immediately, he smiled.

"By chance, were you waiting for me?" he asked.

She shook her head. "I was coming to find you."

"Again?"

"Yes, once again in the same night, I wanted to talk to you."

"*Talk?* Or did you have something else on your mind?"

"As much as I enjoy kissing you, I really need to talk this time, especially after what happened tonight, and what Mrs. Jones... er, *that woman* said."

He nodded. "I suspected as much."

She opened her door wider and let him enter before closing it. "Gavin, please be honest with me and tell me what is going on. You mentioned that someone is stealing your money. Is that true?"

"Indeed, there is a thief in this house, but then again, I don't know who this responsible party is or why and how they are taking my money."

She grasped his hand and pulled him to the sofa. As they both sat, he slid his arm around her shoulders, pulling her closer. She snuggled against him and rested her hand on his chest. No longer was he wearing his waistcoat and cravat. Now he appeared just as comfortable as she was.

"Tell me what is going on."

While he explained about the money that was slowly going missing from his coffers, she could hear the irritation in his voice. She couldn't believe what his father had done, and all that Gavin needed to do in order to repair the family name.

She took his hand and gently squeezed it. "Gavin, I want you to cancel all my dress orders. I don't need new gowns. I can make them myself. And as for those bonnets, first thing in the morning, I will return them. I never did like wearing those cumbersome things on my head, anyway."

His expression softened as his gaze dropped to her mouth. "You deserve new gowns, and I will not have my wife in anything less. As for the bonnets..." He shrugged. "I don't like them on your head either. They hide your lovely hair." He lifted her hand and kissed her knuckles. "However, I don't want you to worry about me. I don't know how, but I will find out who is taking my money, and I'll make them return every shilling. Besides, I will be selling all the other estates in my inheritance, so that will help. We will live here with my grandmother until I have enough to purchase us another home."

"Oh, Gavin. Please, let me help you in some way. I see how frustrated you are with going over the ledgers. I have done this for my father for years. I might be able to see something you aren't."

His shoulders straightened and his wide-eyed gaze locked with hers. "You have done your father's accounts?"

She nodded. "Bridget started them, but then I started helping her, and when she married, I took over."

"Oh, thank the Lord!"

He cupped her face and leaned forward, kissing her quickly. She didn't have time to enjoy it before he pulled away.

"My lovely Cilla, I didn't realize until now what a godsend you are. Tomorrow after breakfast, I will take you to my study and have you look over the ledgers. Perhaps you will see something."

She grinned. "Indeed. After all, an extra pair of eyes can't hurt." Excitement grew inside her. "Gavin, I'm sure we will find something. I would rather toil by your side than have you do it alone."

Sighing, he shook his head. "Is it any wonder I fell in love with you so quickly? You really are remarkable."

She shrugged. "Then we share the same mind, because I feel that way about you."

He wrapped both arms around her, holding her closer as he kissed her passionately. Once again, it wasn't at all what she wanted before he stopped and pulled away. Then again, maybe it was a good thing they didn't kiss to their hearts' content tonight. They would fall asleep doing it.

"My love, I will let you go to sleep now. Tomorrow, I will keep you busy, I promise."

"As long as we are together, I don't care how busy I am."

He kissed her one last time before rising from the sofa and leaving. Finally, she would be able to sleep very well tonight, now that they were being honest with each other. Now she couldn't wait for more sharing, caring, and, especially, loving.

Chapter Eighteen

WHY HAD SHE slept so long? Priscilla hurried through her toilette as soon as she realized it was way past breakfast. She hurried her maid, telling the woman not to mess with her hair. Instead, she wrapped the bulk of Priscilla's hair in a coil and pinned it up nicely. The day dress she picked out was one she had worn earlier in the week, but she didn't care. It wasn't as though she would be entertaining guests. All she planned was to stay in Gavin's study until she noticed a discrepancy in the accounting. She prayed it was easy to spot, since she didn't want to let him down.

Once she was ready, she hurried out of her room and down the grand stairs toward the dining room. When she entered, only the dowager sat at the table, eating her food. She looked up and smiled at Priscilla.

"You are finally awake," the dowager declared. "We feared you would sleep the morning away."

Priscilla groaned. "Forgive me, Your Grace. I had planned on being up earlier, but this time the sun didn't wake me as it usually does."

The dowager chuckled. "That is probably because it's raining, and the clouds have hidden the sun." She motioned to one of the chairs. "Please, sit and have something to eat. You are probably famished."

Priscilla really wanted to see Gavin and help him, but the dowager was correct. She needed to eat in order to keep her mind strong.

"I shall eat, but then, if you don't mind, I need to help your grandson."

The dowager's smile widened. "He did inform me that was what the two of you were planning on doing today, and I commend you for having such knowledge. I must say, most ladies of the *haute ton* would not admit to having that skill."

Priscilla sat and let the servant bring her a plate of food. The heavenly scent of scones with warm honey butter, and ham in some type of sauce, made her stomach growl. She ate, trying not to appear as though she was in a hurry, but she suspected the dowager knew anyway.

She swallowed a mouthful of food before speaking. "Where is the duke now?"

"He is in his study. Mr. Jacob McGuire stopped by unexpectedly, so Gavin took him to the study."

"Who is that?" Priscilla asked as she cut a piece of ham and popped it into her mouth.

"He is Gavin's secretary." The dowager sighed heavily. "It vexes me sorely that my own son would have been such a spendthrift that he gave a depleted inheritance to his own son. Why, if he was still alive right now, I would have everything put back in my name. Gavin certainly didn't deserve it." She huffed. "My son wasn't the perfect father, and he certainly wasn't a good husband, with all the illegitimate children he made. If only I had known about this while my own husband was alive, we might have done something to stop this from happening."

Priscilla nearly choked on her food. *Illegitimate children?* Although shocking, it shouldn't have been a surprise. After all, the royal family had illegitimate offspring all over the country, she was certain.

She quickly sipped her tea, hoping to unclog her throat and, at the same time, try not to look as though she was choking.

"Oh, heavens." The dowager's cheeks brightened with color. "Perhaps I should not have said anything. I can see how the news upsets you, my dear."

Priscilla waved a dismissive hand through the air. "Think nothing of it. Although it is not generally talked about, we all know it happens."

"Well, I haven't said anything to Gavin, but I saw the way he was looking at the girl the other day during my soirée."

Priscilla nearly choked again. "His illegitimate sister was here at your party?"

Frowning, the dowager sighed heavily. "I wasn't certain that Lady Burns had been my son's mistress, and I wanted to get a closer look at the girl, which is why I invited them. Of course, when I realized the remarkable resemblance between Gavin and Georgina, it was too late. But my grandson noticed. I saw him studying the girl closely. And she was obviously named after my son, George."

Miss Georgina? Was that the reason Gavin had been chatting with her outside the dressmaker's shop yesterday? "I can't believe I didn't see the resemblance between them." She paused, not sure if she should ask the next question on her mind but knowing she would, whether it was daring or not. "Do you think Miss Georgina wants Gavin to welcome her in the family?"

"It's just not done. I'm sure the girl is sweet, but she is illegitimate, and that is how it will always be."

"You are correct, of course. I just feel poorly for the young woman, having to go through life without a father."

The dowager wagged her finger at Priscilla. "Don't you feel sorry for her or her mother. I'm quite certain while my son was alive, he gave his mistresses money and paid for their townhouses. As for Miss Georgina not having a father, her stepfather is a nice enough man, so she is just fine."

"Lord Burns? I think I saw him outside the milliner's shop yesterday."

Confusion filled the dowager's expression. "Are you certain it was Lord Burns? The last I heard, the man was lying on his deathbed."

"Oh, well, then maybe it wasn't him. I just saw a man with brown hair talking to Miss Georgina yesterday."

The dowager shook her head. "That wasn't Lord Burns. The poor man is nearly bald by now, and he is in his seventies."

Priscilla finished eating her breakfast as she recalled the conversation she'd overheard between Miss Georgina and the man, thinking it very confusing. But it certainly made Priscilla believe that the young woman was spoiled, no matter her circumstances in life.

After swallowing the last bite, she took the linen napkin and dabbed her mouth. "I hope you will excuse me now. I'm eager to help Gavin."

"Of course, my dear."

Priscilla stood, but quickly stopped. "Do I need to wheel you anywhere before I go?"

The dowager swished her hand through the air. "Miss Priscilla, although I hired you as my companion, rest assured I just wanted womanly company. Martin has been pushing me around in my rollerchair for years. I shall be fine."

Priscilla laughed and quickly left the room. She didn't mind hearing that the dowager didn't really need her. Apparently, fate had lent them both a helping hand.

She really shouldn't run, but her steps were faster than they should be as she rushed toward the study. Turning the corner, she noticed a man walk out of the room, saying something to Gavin as he stepped into the corridor. It wasn't until the man faced her that she recognized him as the man whom Miss Georgina had been visiting with yesterday.

Immediately, her mind filled in the missing puzzle pieces. Gavin had told her money was missing from his account, but didn't have any idea how it was happening—but he expected it was someone who lived on the estate. Then there was that awkward conversation yesterday between Miss Georgina and Mr.

McGuire.

Her legs stopped moving as she stared at the man walking toward her. He gave her a nod before passing.

Words were lodged in her throat, and she didn't want to believe any of it. Yet what else could it be? Mr. McGuire would have access to Gavin's money, and it seemed he was giving it to Gavin's illegitimate, spoiled sister.

"There you are." Gavin's voice boomed through the air.

She swung her attention toward him as he came toward her. His smile widened more the closer he came.

"Before you say anything, I didn't have the heart to let the maid wake you." He stopped in front of her and caressed her cheek. "Do you forgive me?"

"I... I..." She swallowed hard. "Gavin, we must talk. Now."

Without waiting for his answer, she grabbed his arm, practically pulled him into the study, and closed the door. She pointed toward the hall.

"The person stealing your money just left this room," she declared, not knowing how else to tell him.

Gavin's eyes narrowed. He didn't look at her as though he didn't believe her, but she couldn't exactly tell what he might be thinking. He stared at her without saying a thing and blinked several times. She hoped he was just surprised at her statement.

"You see," she continued, "I saw Mr. McGuire in front of the milliner's shop yesterday, talking to Miss Georgina, and I overheard a little of their conversation. Yesterday, it didn't make any sense, but after your grandmother told me who Miss Georgina *really* is, and after seeing your secretary leave the study just now, the conversation I overheard makes sense."

Gavin inhaled a shaky breath and squared his shoulders. "Tell me what you heard."

She proceeded to tell Gavin about Miss Georgina's spoiled antics of wanting a new gown and pushing Mr. McGuire to get her the money before the balls she would attend. Priscilla tried to remember the conversation word for word, but knew she was probably missing something. Still, she was able to get the general idea across.

Gavin shook his head and moved back behind his desk to sit. He stared down at the open ledgers on his desk. "Why couldn't I see it?"

"Because Mr. McGuire didn't want you to."

She moved beside him and touched his shoulder. Leaning forward slightly, she skimmed over the open page. Immediately, she noticed a spot and pointed to the line.

"See right here? He logged in an amount on April 14. The next day, he wrote another amount, but had already subtracted one hundred pounds. So when you add up these columns, you don't see it written down as an expense."

Cursing, Gavin raked his fingers through his hair. "All this time? Jacob has been stealing from me since I took over as duke?"

"Actually, I wouldn't doubt that he was stealing from your father as well."

Gavin snorted a forced laugh. "And the weak man was probably too intoxicated to notice what his secretary was doing." He looked up at her. "But why would he do that?"

"I don't know for certain why, but Miss Georgina is definitely involved."

He covered his face with his hands and leaned his elbows on the desk. "I trusted him, and I'm sure my father did as well."

"There has to be a connection." She rubbed his neck with both of her hands. "We just need to find out what."

He sat up again, took her wrist, and led her around to sit on his lap. The moment was intimate, and her heartbeat raced. Now was certainly not the time to feel this way, but how could she not when they were in this position?

"Priscilla Hartwell? What would I do without you?"

She chuckled. "Do you really want me to answer that?"

"No, because I already know." He cupped the side of her face. "I feel foolish for not noticing the discrepancy myself, but I suppose I didn't want to suspect Jacob, so I put the doubt from my mind."

"You are not a fool for thinking he was innocent. After all, he was your friend as well as your father's."

"Tell me, my love. How do I prove that he is the thief?"

"We can go to the bank. They will know if Mr. McGuire has taken out funds in your name."

He chuckled again, but this time it wasn't forced. "Once again, you are proving how intelligent you are. Indeed, you are one in a million. No other woman is like you."

She grinned. "Flattery will get you anything you want."

He arched an eyebrow. "Anything?"

"Of course, but may I suggest you not collect that here in your study?" She glanced around the room. "It doesn't look too comfortable."

His laughter warmed her heart as he hugged her tightly. "I think I grow to love you more and more each day."

"And I you." She bent and kissed his mouth, but when he tried to deepen the kiss, she withdrew. "May I suggest we take a ride to the bank and talk to someone there? I would hate to have anything distract us from our goal."

"You are a wicked woman, aren't you?"

"I love to tease, if that is what you're asking. Then again, so do you."

"I think my bad habits are rubbing off on you." He winked.

"I welcome the rubbing… any way I can get it."

Chapter Nineteen

GAVIN TAPPED HIS hand nervously against his thigh as he sat at the table and stared out the window. Across the street was the bank his family had used for as long as he could remember. This was the place that had been designated to keep his money safe. But it wasn't their fault they kept giving it to Jacob McGuire, the so-called trusted employee.

Inwardly, Gavin boiled with anger. How could he have been so blind? He understood how his father had looked past Jacob's insubordination, since the intoxicated man never knew which way was up. If only Gavin could figure out why Jacob had been stealing from their coffers all these years.

Sitting next to him at the table, Priscilla slipped her hand over his and squeezed. He moved his focus from the bank and looked at her. She was absolutely the most perfect woman he had ever met, and so lovely to look upon.

"Things will work out," she said. "I just know it."

Smiling, he exhaled deeply, wondering if he had been breathing at all these past several minutes. The tension was thick in the air, and growing even thicker.

"My love, although you have opened my eyes to what McGuire has been doing, I don't know what possessed me to bring you with me."

She chuckled. "You had no other choice. I wasn't about to

allow you to do this alone."

He lifted her hand to his mouth and tenderly kissed her knuckles. "You are the only thing that will calm me right now. I thank you for believing in me the way you do."

"Now you must believe in the constable and the bank. Because of their plan to capture Mr. McGuire and Miss Georgina, I trust that they will be arrested this morning."

Although he found strength in Priscilla's positive thinking, he still had doubts. Yesterday, when they went into the bank to inquire about Jacob's frequent visits to withdraw banknotes, Gavin discovered that his secretary had been taking his money once a month. The bank's staff hadn't thought anything was amiss, since Jacob had been doing this since before Gavin became the duke.

After gathering that information, Gavin took Priscilla with him to visit the constable and report his findings. That was when they devised a plan. They would have the bank place a marking on one of the banknotes before handing it over to Jacob. Then, Gavin and Priscilla would sit across the street at the Tea Room shop and watch as Jacobs entered the bank. Once the man left, they would follow him until he gave Miss Georgina the money. The constable would also be on the lookout and make the arrests.

It seemed so easy, but Gavin *knew* something would happen to make the plan crumble. Misfortune wasn't about to leave his life so easily.

He kissed her knuckles again. "If you believe, then I must."

"Gavin," she said in a whisper, "we will capture these thieves one way or another. Now that we know who they are and how Mr. McGuire is taking the money, they will soon be brought to justice."

He nodded. "I think the wait will indeed kill me. I'm not a patient man."

"Then may I suggest that you stare into my eyes as we discuss other things?"

He grinned. "What did you have in mind, my love?"

"Whatever your heart desires," she said.

"Oh, there is only one thing I desire from you, but alas, we must wait until after we are married." He winked. "But I wouldn't mind practicing a little before that happy day arrives."

She laughed. "You are impossible, but that is why I adore you."

She glanced toward the bank, and he peered out the window again. When the familiar man walked up the street and into the bank, Gavin's heartbeat quickened with anticipation and nervousness.

"There he is." He nodded toward the bank without looking at Priscilla. "Do you know how difficult it is not to rush over there and punch the man in the face myself?"

"I can only imagine." She patted his hand. "But we must be patient if we are going to capture both thieves."

The minutes ticked by so slowly that Gavin wondered if the clock in the Tea Room had stopped. He pulled out his timepiece from his pocket to double-check. Finally, after ten very long and agonizing minutes, Jacob left the bank.

Gavin jumped up from his chair so fast it nearly toppled to the floor. He took Priscilla's hand, and they left the shop. Trying to keep a considerable distance between them and Jacob, Gavin walked slowly, even if his heart was jumping.

The constable was up the street, and although Gavin couldn't see him, he must have confidence that that man also had his eyes on Jacob. But even if the constable didn't, Gavin was determined to make this right. He wanted his money back, even if he doubted they had it all. But stopping future transactions would be just as satisfying.

Jacob took a leisurely stroll as if he didn't have a care in the world. Of course, why would the man suspect he was being followed? He hadn't been caught stealing all this time, so why now?

"Where do you think he is heading?" Priscilla asked.

"I would think he is meeting Miss Georgina somewhere out

in the open so as not to arouse suspicion with people seeing them together."

"Do you think they are in love?"

Gavin snorted a laugh. "For as long as the man has been stealing from my family and giving it to Miss Georgina, I doubt they are in love. She was probably a child when McGuire first stole from my father."

It surprised Gavin when Jacob slowed and walked into the park. He released Priscilla's hand but hooked it around his elbow so that they appeared more natural. A handful of couples strolled along the green lawns and blossoming flower gardens. He tried to search for Miss Georgina, but he didn't want to take his eyes off Jacob for very long.

"Do you see her?" he asked Priscilla.

"Not yet."

A few times, Jacob stopped to visit with park patrons. Gavin and Priscilla also stopped and acted like they were enjoying the flowers, but he wouldn't let Jacob out of his sight. He could see that Jacob searched for someone. Gavin was grateful the man didn't notice him and Priscilla in the park—but even if he did, why would he suspect they were following him? Acting as if nothing was happening would be the key to capturing the man.

"There she is," Priscilla whispered. "She is with her mother."

Gavin led Priscilla under the canopy branches of a tree. It was easier to spy on Jacob this way. Gavin didn't care if tongues would wag because he was alone with his mother's companion. They would be married soon, anyway.

It surprised him when he noticed the look of admiration on Jacob's face when he stared at Lady Burns. Although the woman had been married all of her daughter's life, Gavin had always wondered if she was truly in love with her husband, since he was much older. And now Gavin could see her tender expression of love as her gaze met Jacob.

"They are in love," Gavin whispered to Priscilla.

"That still doesn't explain why Mr. McGuire was stealing

your family's money."

"My guess is that he felt sorry for his lady love because my father found a different mistress when he discovered she was pregnant. I think Jacob could have loved her even while she was my father's mistress, and once she was discarded, he wanted to take care of her and her unborn child."

"Then why didn't she marry Mr. McGuire?"

Gavin shrugged. "Perhaps he didn't think he could provide for them. But with Lady Burns being with child, she would have to find a husband quickly to prevent scandal. In that case, an older man seeking a wife was the one to search for. I'm quite certain Lord Burns didn't even know he wasn't Georgina's father."

"It's quite sad, actually."

He glanced at Priscilla. She had such a kind heart. "Why do you think it's sad?"

"Because she couldn't marry the man she truly loved." Priscilla touched his face. "Eighteen months ago, I knew I was falling in love with you, but I feared you wouldn't want me for a wife because of my lowly circumstances. Even now, I wonder why you want to marry me, considering I don't have a dowry."

"Oh, my lovely Cilla." He covered her hand resting on his cheek. "Sometimes men fall in love whether they want to or not. If you recall, I hadn't wanted to marry, but once I got to know you, I realized no other woman would make me as happy as you have made me."

She smiled, and her blue eyes twinkled. "You say the sweetest words."

"That is because I'm a man in love, and I don't care if you are the king's daughter or the child of an unmarried woman. You are the one for me."

As much as he wanted nothing more than to hold her and shower her with passionate kisses, that would have to wait. Right now, he needed to watch Jacob closely.

Gavin switched his gaze back to his secretary and Mrs. Burns. As they chatted, they both looked happy. Unfortunately, the spoiled young woman beside them appeared to be quite bored, as she folded her arms and tapped a foot. Georgina's scowl let him know Jacob hadn't handed over the money yet. If so, the young woman would be rushing to the nearest dressmaker's shop.

He exhaled slowly, trying to be patient. He had made it this far without punching the man in the face. He could wait a little longer.

Gavin glanced at the flower bush closest to them. Daisies were in full bloom, reminding him of that afternoon when Priscilla and Grams were in her garden by the flowers. He quickly picked a daisy and handed it to her.

"Thank you, my love, for helping me with this issue. I don't know what I would have done without you."

Smiling, she lifted the daisy to her nose and sniffed. "I'm very happy to help in any way I can."

He wanted to gaze into her eyes forever, but he glanced again at the threesome standing together. Finally, Jacob reached inside his waistcoat and pulled out a stack of banknotes. Georgina snatched them quickly and stuffed them in her wrist purse.

Gavin searched the area for the constable but couldn't see him. Where was the man? This was the perfect time to make the arrests.

"Cilla, we might have to confront them," he said.

"Why?"

"I don't see the constable." He scanned the park again as irritation built inside his chest.

Priscilla gasped. "Oh dear. Miss Georgina is leaving with her mother."

Gavin switched his focus back to the two women. They were indeed leaving while Jacob walked in a different direction.

"Who should we follow?" Priscilla asked.

"Lady Burns and her self-centered daughter, since she is the one with the marked banknotes."

"But what about Mr. McGuire?"

Gavin shook his head. "We cannot worry about him now.

The staff at the bank will attest that he picked up the marked banknote. That will get him arrested."

He hooked Priscilla's arm around his elbow again, but this time they couldn't appear as though they were taking a leisurely stroll through the park, especially when Georgina's steps were hurried. It was difficult not to draw attention to themselves, but he wasn't about to let his illegitimate sister—or her greedy mother—get away with this.

As soon as the mother and daughter exited the park, they headed toward Madame Dupont's shop. Gavin didn't know what he would do if they entered, but he wasn't about to let her spend his money.

Georgina slowed down, which made her mother's steps falter. Then the young woman glanced over her shoulder. When her gaze landed on Gavin, her eyes widened.

He cursed under his breath. *She knows!*

The thief lifted the hem of her day dress and sprinted away from her mother, startling the older woman.

Gavin grumbled. *Oh, no you don't!* "Stay here," he told Priscilla before running after his father's other child.

He couldn't believe how fast she was as she darted around people on the street, and even ran across the road, nearly getting hit by a passing carriage. That didn't slow him down. After all, her dress would slow her steps, whereas he had nothing to keep him from moving quickly.

She turned down a side street and, once again, ran across without looking. He wondered why she hadn't gotten hit yet. But he followed, making sure he didn't get run over by a horse or carriage.

Once he was away from the congestion, he searched for her bright yellow dress. She was gone.

Panic flowed through him with every breath he took. He couldn't have lost her now. But she wasn't out in plain sight. That meant she had ducked in one of the nearest shops. However, he didn't have time to check all of them. He needed her found. Now!

The piercing shrill of a whistle could be heard in the distance. He glanced over his shoulder to see the constable and two bobbies running toward him. Finally, he would get some help.

Gavin waved to the lawmen. "I lost her somewhere around here," he shouted.

While they went into the shops to look, Gavin moved slowly up the street. She had disappeared so fast that he was certain she was close by. When he came to the first alley, instinct told him to head in that direction.

With each step, he listened closely, hoping to hear something that indicated her whereabouts. As he made it to the end of the alley, he stopped. His breathing came rushed, but he couldn't allow that to cease his search.

A woman's angered scream shook the air around him, and he hurried from around the building. Not far from him stood Priscilla blocking a woman wearing a bright yellow dress.

"I demand you move aside," Georgina snapped as she glared at Priscilla.

His lovely bride-to-be stood not far in front of Georgina, holding a broom in her hand. Although it wasn't much of a weapon, he was certain his Cilla wouldn't have a qualm about knocking it against Georgina's head.

"You can demand all you want for all the good it will do." Priscilla lifted her chin stubbornly.

"Who do you think you are, treating me like that? Why, you're just a lady's companion."

Gavin gritted his teeth. How dare she treat a *real* lady like that? "And you," he said loudly, getting her attention as she swung toward him, "are nothing but the daughter of a duke's mistress. The way I see it, Miss Priscilla has every right to talk to you in such a manner. You, however, have no right to talk to my future wife that way."

Georgina's mouth dropped open in shock. "You are going to marry her?"

Gavin chuckled as he walked closer. "You're not the imbecile

I first thought you to be." He rolled his eyes. "Miss Priscilla and I are engaged. But that is not your concern now." He pointed to her wrist purse. "You, your awful mother, and my *former* secretary, Mr. McGuire, have been stealing my money. It will stop now."

She turned up her nose at him. "I haven't any idea what you are referring to, Your Grace."

"I beg to differ." He motioned toward her purse again. "The proof of your crime is in there."

"Your Grace, really. This needs to stop. You are accusing an innocent woman."

"Are you telling me you don't threaten Mr. McGuire to get money from me so that you can have new gowns?" He arched an eyebrow. "Miss Priscilla will attest to overhearing you and my former secretary discussing that very subject yesterday in front of the milliner's shop. We have already talked to the constable, and if necessary, we shall get the Birmingham police involved as well."

Her innocent expression quickly turned to hatred as she glared at him. "This was your father's fault. He was the one who turned away and wouldn't do anything to help my mother once she was with child. Then *you*." She flipped her hand toward him. "You told me in your own words that you would never welcome an illegitimate child into the family."

"And if you believe otherwise, then you were the one who was mistaken. It's just not done. If so, there would be many royal children who were not mothered by the queen."

Suddenly, the constable and two bobbies rushed around the corner of the building, but they stopped when they saw Gavin. He pointed to Georgina. "Check her wrist purse. You will locate the marked banknote there."

The bobbies apprehended Georgina, and although she struggled, the constable was able to get into her wrist purse and find the marked note.

Relief flooded Gavin. Finally, this was over.

"What about Lady Burns?" Priscilla asked.

"Not to worry, Miss Priscilla," one of the bobbies said. "We already caught her."

The constable nodded. "Our next stop will be to catch Mr. McGuire."

"You will find him at one of the gentlemen's clubs, I believe," Gavin informed them.

The constable nodded. "Thank you, Your Grace."

"I appreciate your assistance." Gavin walked closer to Priscilla. When he reached her side, she leaned against him, smiling.

"It is done. You no longer need to worry about them stealing your money."

"If not for you, I would still be in this mess." He caressed her chin. "Now I can concentrate on our wedding."

"And when will that be?"

He grinned. "Tomorrow, if I can arrange it."

"But Gavin, I think there might have been some miscommunication about that."

Confusion filled him. "What do you mean?"

"You have never proposed. In fact, you only *told* me we were getting married."

Tilting back his head, he laughed heartily. He loved how she made him so lighthearted. But she was correct. He needed to propose.

He took her hands and knelt in front of her, staring up into her gorgeous blue eyes. "Miss Priscilla, will you do me the honor of becoming my wife, the mother of my children, and my lifelong companion as we seek new adventures every day?"

Her eyes twinkled with mirth. "Every day for the rest of our lives? That is a very long time, my love."

"It is, but it will be well worth it, I assure you."

She nodded, grinning widely. "Then I accept your proposal, but only because I love you so much I don't think I could live without you."

He stood and gathered her in his arms. "Then it's settled.

Since neither of us can live without the other, we should indeed marry, and quickly. If you keep kissing me with such passion, I'm not sure how long I can remain a gentleman."

"Then what do you say we spend the rest of the day seeing how quickly we can plan our wedding?"

"I would say you were a very wise woman."

Epilogue

Priscilla's heart was overflowing with emotion today, and she cried over everything. She'd never thought she would be this happy, and she'd absolutely never imagined she would have such a grand wedding, especially since she and Gavin were *forced* to have it quickly.

All of her sisters had attended, along with her father and grandmother. Grandmama was overjoyed to see her best friend, the Dowager Duchess of Englewood. Many of Gavin's friends, and most of his cousins, were also in attendance. Priscilla suspected his cousins came because they doubted he would go through with it, but thankfully, Gavin did.

She was welcomed wholeheartedly into the Worthington family, and she couldn't count how many times she heard someone say that they were grateful that Gavin had found a woman to love and who would love him back completely.

She couldn't stop staring at her new husband. He was so incredibly handsome, and she was certain she would always find herself staring at him dreamily. He looked even better now, only because his gaze was filled with such longing and desire. There was no doubt what was on his mind. It was on her mind, too.

"It's so very hard to accept that you're a married woman," Felicia whined teasingly as she hooked her arm around Priscilla's. "I miss the days when we were younger and causing problems around town."

Priscilla arched an eyebrow. "*We?* Felicia, I believe you don't remember our childhood as Bridget and I do. It was you and Jannette who caused all the problems. Bridget and I were angels."

Felicia snorted a laugh. "I wouldn't exactly call you two *angels*." She nodded. "But you're probably right that Nettie and I gave our father more headaches than you and Bridget ever did."

Priscilla chuckled. *"Probably?* No, dearest sister, there is no question about that."

"Oh, you know me. I hate to admit when I'm wrong."

"That is the truth, but Felicia, it's something you must overcome. Men do not like a woman who thinks she is always right."

Felicia rolled her eyes. "But therein lies the problem. You see, most of the time, I *am* always right." She shrugged. "I just enjoy pointing it out to them."

Priscilla laughed. "Oh, my dear, wayward sister. Believe me when I tell you that you are *not* always right. And men do enjoy hearing a woman admit when she is wrong."

She glanced around the groups of people and spotted Gavin. "Felicia, I hope you will forgive me, but I need to talk to my husband now."

"Of course." Felicia hugged her and walked away.

Priscilla headed in her husband's direction. Gavin was talking to some of his cousins, but when he saw her walking toward him, he quickly excused himself and met her halfway. Grinning widely, he gathered her loosely in his arms.

"So, my sweet duchess, are you ready to leave this party and start our lives together? I cannot wait to get you alone, because this time, it won't be scandalous." He waggled his eyebrows.

Her heart melted that much more. She was so pleased that he had changed for the better. Eighteen months ago, when he was a rogue, he would have never thought of anyone but himself, and he definitely wouldn't have sought her opinions or wishes, as he did now. She loved how he included her in everything.

She sighed dreamily. "I love you, Gavin, and I'm anticipating when we can start our lives as man and wife. I pray you will never tire of me."

He caressed her cheek. "How can I tire of someone I admire? Cilla, I plan on keeping you with me forever."

"Could I love you any more?" She smiled.

"I'm sure you could, just as I could love you more. Every day as your husband will make me completely happy."

"Gavin?" she asked softly.

"Yes, my love?"

"Is it permissible to kiss you in front of every—"

He placed his mouth over hers before she could finish speaking. She hitched a breath, but it didn't take long before she kissed him back. Perhaps this was scandalous, but at least the gossipmongers would know how much she loved this man.

Was there anything better in life than loving someone with all of her heart?

She thought not.

THE END

Other published stories by Marie Higgins
www.authormariehiggins.com/books

Join my newsletter and start your reading collection
www.authormariehiggins.com/newsletter

About the Author

Marie Higgins is an award-winning, best-selling author of clean romance novels that melt your heart and have you falling in love over and over again. Since 2010, she's published over 100 heartwarming, on-the-edge-of-your-seat romances. She has broadened her readership by writing mystery/suspense, humor, time travel, and paranormal, along with her love for historical romances. Her readers have dubbed her "Queen of Tease" because of all her twists and unexpected endings.

Website – www.authormariehiggins.com
Facebook – facebook.com/marie.higgins.7543
TikTok – tiktok.com/@author.mariehiggins
Instagram – instagram.com/author.mariehiggins
Bookbub – bookbub.com/authors/marie-higgins

Milton Keynes UK
Ingram Content Group UK Ltd.
UKHW021955120424
441050UK00013B/459

9 781963 585391